DEAR BOY

Bibliography

Chesterfield and His Critics by Roger Coxon (London, 1925)

Lord Chesterfield by Samuel Shellabarger (London, 1935)

The True Chesterfield by Willard Connely (London, 1939)

On Hagakure by Yukio Mishima (Penguin, 1979)

Republican Party Reptile by P.J. O'Rourke (Picador, 1987)

The History of Manners by Norbert Elias (Oxford, 1978)

English Society in the 18th Century by Roy Porter (Pelican, 1982)

Englishmen and Manners in the 18th Century by A.S. Turberville (Oxford, 1929)

Johnson's England by A.S. Turberville (Oxford, 1933)

References to the above are generally made in the text by means of the author's surname only.

DEAR BOY

LORD CHESTERFIELD'S LETTERS TO HIS SON

INTRODUCED BY
CATHERINE COOKSON

BANTAM PRESS

LONDON · NEW YORK · TORONTO · SYDNEY · AUCKLAND

TRANSWORLD PUBLISHERS LTD
61-63 Uxbridge Road, London W5 5SA

TRANSWORLD PUBLISHERS (AUSTRALIA) PTY LTD
15-23 Helles Avenue, Moorebank, NSW 2170

TRANSWORLD PUBLISHERS (NZ) LTD
Cnr Moselle and Waipareira Aves,
Henderson, Auckland

Published 1989 by Bantam Press
a division of Transworld Publishers Ltd
Copyright © Pilot Productions Ltd 1989
Introduction copyright © Catherine Cookson 1989

Edited by
Piers Dudgeon and Jonathan Jones

Illustrated by
Paul Cox

Design concept by
Mike McGuinness

British Library Cataloguing in Publication Data
Chesterfield, Philip Dormer Stanhope. Earl of, 1694-1773
Dear boy: a strategy for rising in the world.
I. Title 826′.6

ISBN 0-593-01790-0

Typeset in
Ehrhardt by Dorchester Typesetting Ltd,
Dorset, England

Printed by
Printer Portuguesa Grafica Lda, Portugal

CONTENTS

Who Was Lord Chesterfield?   6

Introduction by Catherine Cookson   13

Chapter One: Born to Success?   30

Chapter Two: The Art of Learning   35

Chapter Three: Make the World Your
                Schoolroom   52

Chapter Four: Attend, Observe, Imitate   70

Chapter Five: Style – Pleasing the Eyes
                and the Ears   87

Chapter Six: Making Friends and
                Influencing People   120

Chapter Seven: Business Strategy   133

Chapter Eight: The Art of Negotiation   148

Chapter Nine: The Utility of Moral Sense   165

Chapter Ten: The Art of Performance   174

WHO WAS LORD CHESTERFIELD?

P hilip Dormer Stanhope, the 4th Earl of Chesterfield was born on 22nd September, 1694. In Catherine Cookson's words, 'Chesterfield's father, the 3rd Earl, was a rake, a kind of man who apparently never grew up.' The 3rd Earl shunned his wife, who died when she was thirty-three after bearing him nine sons (of whom Philip was the second), and went off to France. Philip was brought up by his grandmother, Gertrude Pierrepont, the Marchioness of Halifax, and she set him on the path to success. She saw to it that he had a good education certainly, but as important she taught him what in those days were known as the Graces and might today be called social skills or style. He went to Cambridge University and by nineteen was learned, witty, a great orator, a gambler known for his 'high play', and despite a fairly hideous appearance, he was popular with the ladies.

Chesterfield entered Parliament in 1715 but after a highly successful maiden speech was challenged by a member of the Opposition, who pointed out that he was not yet twenty-one and too young to represent his constituency. Chesterfield stepped down until he came of age, wiling away the time as Gentleman of the Bed Chamber to the Prince of Wales. Once he became an active politician he did well, although one suspects he would have done better had he not delighted in putting down those who were at one time or another favourites of the King or Queen. He became Ambassador to the Hague, then Lord Lieutenant of Ireland where, through tact and good judgment, he achieved much in a very short space of time. Finally, he became Secretary of State to the Foreign Office, before retiring at fifty-three with rheumatic gout and increasing deafness.

When Ambassador to the Hague he conceived a son with a woman called Madelena Elizabeth du Bouchet. The boy, also named Philip, was born in 1732. Chesterfield saw to it that he was well educated. He sent him to Westminster School, thence to the Universities of Lousanne and Leipsig and finally on an extended European tour to France, Germany, Switzerland and Italy under the protection of a full-time tutor and with introductions to the best society in all the capitals.

The *Letters* were written by Chesterfield to his son from 1739 (the main body of this selection being written during his Grand Tour), and continued through Philip's career as politician (he was elected twice to Parliament) and his diplomatic appointments in Hamburg, Ratisbon and Dresden, until his untimely death at the age of thirty-six.

In a symbolic sense, the letters – patronly, sometimes avuncular in tone, and full of good advice – espouse a connection between father and son that Philip's illegitimacy called into question. Indeed they may perhaps be said to represent an attempt by Chesterfield to rest a finger on the basic roulette of fate, which had spun the boy a poor return at birth. They concern education in the narrow sense very little; they were written to supplement Philip's academic education with wise words from a man of the world.

When they first appeared in book form in 1774, one year after Lord Chesterfield's death, they met with instant success: five editions appeared before the end of the year. But the initial take-up was not due to Chesterfield's reputation as a man of deep genius (which he was not) or to his political success, rather to his public perception as a man of social ingenuity and wit, and his 'perfect knowledge of mankind'.

For historians, the letters offer an extraordinary insight into the habits of the day, the temper of the Age of Reason. But their interest two centuries on, goes far beyond an historical

'It is of great use to a young man, before he sets out for that country, full of mazes, windings, and turnings, to have at least a general map of it, made by some experienced traveller.'

appreciation. They provide a strategy for success which transcends the passage of time.

The traditional English prejudice against success found a voice in Chesterfield's critics of the 18th and 19th Centuries, who seized upon his philosophy of self-interest and the frankness (some would say cynicism) with which he expressed it. Echoes of dissent call into question how Britain's best-loved author, Catherine Cookson, could deliver up the reason for her own achievement to a man who has been described as having 'the mien of a posture-maker, the skin-deep graciousness of a French Marechal. . .a calculating adventurer who cuts unpretentious worthies to toady to society magnates, who affects the supercilious air of a shallow dandy and cherishes the heart of a frog.' Perhaps the answer lies both in the appalling circumstances in which Catherine found herself as a young woman and in a more enlightened appreciation of what Chesterfield actually advised. Certainly, she proved the efficacy of his advice.

Catherine Cookson was born in 1906 into the bleak industrial heartland of Tyneside, the illegitimate daughter of a barmaid who gave over her life to drink, and a man she never met. Catherine's childhood was spent in abject poverty, fetching beer to feed her mother's habit, going to the pawn shop to balance the family's precarious existence, and following the coke carts to pick up the overspill for oven and fire. At fourteen she left school and started working as a maid, and later as a seamstress in the laundry at Harton Workhouse.

In her Introduction to *Dear Boy*, Catherine Cookson tells how Chesterfield gave her the confidence and wherewithal to drag herself out of the mire, to come to terms with the stigma of her own illegitimacy, to rise above her misfortune while remaining true to her roots, and, eventually, by his example, to write without pretension and with a naturalness which released in her a talent that has led to her becoming this country's most successful living writer. She shows too how he helped her as much when she became successful and took on the duties of the public figure (moving in new circles, public speaking, and so on). 'I had a mentor,' she recalls, 'a friend; and the fact that I was in the same boat as his son drew me closer to him.'

How then does Catherine's experience marry with the Machiavellian image of a man who co-erces his son to 'pry into the recesses of others' hearts and heads'. . . 'to bait your hook to catch them', to 'flatter people behind their backs, in the presence of those who will not fail to repeat, or even amplify, the praise to the party concerned'? How can she now advocate tutelage at the hands of a man who commends us – of necessity, of utility – to 'preserve the appearances of Religion and Morality', who states that 'without some dissimulation no business can be carried on at all', and who holds that 'a man of the world must, like the chameleon, be able to take every different hue'?

Clues lie in Catherine's purpose in presenting this edition. Like Chesterfield, her first purpose is to share her experience of life: 'I am going off the stage, you are coming upon it,' he wrote to his son in October, 1748. 'With me, what has been, has been, and reflection now would come too late; with you, everything is to come, even, in some manner, reflection itself; so that this is the very time when my reflections, the result of experience, may be of use to you, by supplying the want of yours.'

Her second purpose is to make available an edition of the *Letters* which provides an accessible strategy for present-day readers, a selection which illuminates the practical points of Chesterfield's worldy wisdom and highlights the contexts in which his 'Machiavellian' propositions are made. For example, moral virtue is actually a key concept in Chesterfield's strategy for success: 'For God's sake, be scrupulously jealous of the purity of your moral character,' he writes. While he recommends dissimulation in business – 'not straightway laying all your trump cards on the table' – he distinguishes it from simulation, which is deceit.

Chesterfield's advice always flows from his own experience as politician: 'If in negotiations you are looked upon as a liar, and a trickster, no confidence will be placed in you, nothing will be communicated to you, and you will be in the situation of a man who has been burnt in the cheek; and who, from that mark, cannot afterwards get an honest livelihood if he would, but must continue a thief.'

Again, he recommends the chameleon as model because it is common sense for the aspiring diplomat, 'to adapt your conversation to the people you are conversing with'. 'Bating your hook' may be a provocative expression, but turns on a realistic assessment of the political jungle into which his son intends to launch himself, not on slyness or cunning. He does not set out to train his son in the role of moral reformer. 'We must take things as they are, we cannot make them what we would, nor often what they should be.'

What emerges from his letters is that moral rectitude is essential but that it is as indisputably justified by how things actually go on in the world, as by any precepts of religion: 'There is nothing so delicate as your moral character, and nothing which it is your interest so much to preserve pure. Should you be suspected of injustice, malignity, perfidy, lying, etc., all the parts and knowledge in the world will never procure you esteem, friendship or respect.'

In short, Chesterfield proves moral values at the altar of Reason not Religion. His critics – advocates of Reason to a man – failed to grasp the nettle of their Age and were stung by their own hypocrisy.

INTRODUCTION BY
CATHERINE COOKSON

Why did I become an advocate for Chesterfield? It would have been understandable if after a sound education I had gone to University, and Lord Chesterfield had become my mentor and his period my platform for the study of politics, morals, and manners of the 18th Century. But the opposite was the case.

Here was a girl, a child born illegitimate, who had had a rough time of it from as far back as she could remember when she was three years old, until she was fourteen when she stopped going for the beer or to the pawn, when she stopped following the coke carts on the East Jarrow road in order to pick up the overspill from them, all the time experiencing an inordinate fear of drink, especially of a woman in drink, and gradually becoming aware that she had two sides to her character: first, that she possessed a sensitivity that heightened pain and fear; secondly, that the knowledge that had been revealed to her when she was seven that she was illegitimate brewed an aggressiveness. However, being but a child she was not to become aware of its source for some time. Not until she was fourteen and went into daily service did she realise that she was different, and so acted accordingly.

Now I ask you, was there anything in that early background that would lead her to become a student of Philip Dormer Stanhope, the fourth Earl of Chesterfield? I would say there was nothing. But she was entering her teens and it was during the following six years that the foundation for her passion was laid.

I remained in service for a year. At first I didn't mind being in service, I was earning nine shillings and sixpence a week for cleaning, cooking, and washing for a grown-up family of five. But a year was long enough. There was an unrest in me and I wanted to work for myself, so I took up a little business of pen-painting.

I've explained all this in my autobiography, but it is worth iterating to any young people who might read this that I sat at a table under the window in the kitchen from eight to ten hours a day filling in a pattern of a basket of flowers on a satin cushion cover with oil paints applied with the nib of a pen, five days a week. Saturday was given over to collecting the club money for the said cushions, part of the Sunday I would spend making the articles. Again I made nine shillings and sixpence a week. But after two years and the benefit of contracting lead poisoning I was forced to give up this business.

I went into service again; but this time within a fortnight realisation came that I wasn't made for that kind of service. So, in the autumn of 1924, I found myself engaged as a laundry checker in the South Shields Workhouse.

At that time I was a strong Catholic and I imagined that this was what God intended me to be, a checker in a workhouse laundry. It appeared to be a marvellous job, two pounds a month and all found. However, this feeling of thankfulness to the Deity quickly faded and after a few months I came to the conclusion that He was wrong, for I began to feel I was worth something better. What was I to do about it? Write?

I was quite positive I was a writer. I had started when I was eleven and by the time I was fifteen I had achieved a sixteen thousand word story, which the Shields Daily Gazette had turned down flatly. But besides this firm knowledge of my literary ability there was something I craved and that was, I dearly wanted to be a lady and talk proper.

Now at that time I did not think of the word 'education', the word prominent in my mind being 'culture', because I knew that ladies had to have culture, and culture had something to do with the arts. So what did I do? I went out and bought a second-hand fiddle. I paid ten shillings for it. It was in a case, with a bow and a lump of resin. Then I took lessons at a shilling a time.

This form of culture went on for as long as two quarters, when I discovered there was something wrong with the violin: I couldn't play it. But never daunted in my search for culture, I then took up French; before I could speak English I took up French! Again things did not go my way. It was the teacher this time: she wasn't any good; she couldn't get my Northern accent right. In some despair now I took up physical culture, this with the hope of getting rid of my puppy fat and of developing a beautiful body. The purpose of the beautiful body, if this form of culture was to do its work, was to ensure I caught a rich husband . . . no nice thoughts for a Catholic girl.

I was twenty at the time and a reader of novels, particularly those of Ethel M. Dell, Charles Garvis, Warwick Deeping, Ouida, Arnold Bennett and such like. But there came into my hands one day a book entitled, *The Career of Catherine Bush* by Elinor Glyn. Now, I had never read anything by Elinor Glyn because she was banned by the Catholic Church. Well, what could you expect when she wrote about naked women lying on bear skins. However I read this book and I can say it was from this time that my life changed, and utterly.

Over the years I have come to think that Elinor Glyn was put on this earth mainly to write that book in order to show an ignorant North Country girl the path she must take.

I won't go into the whole story – that would mean writing another book – except to say that the heroine became secretary to a duchess and that the duchess had a friend who was a duke. He was much younger than her and at one time had been more than a friend. But now he visits her on a friendly basis, and during one of these visits who does he see but her secretary; and when talking to her he discovers she is highly intelligent, and, because the story is a romance, he falls in love with her. The duchess was incensed, and although she was very fond of Catherine Bush and had come to accept that she was a special person, nevertheless, she was of the common people and the duke was of the aristocracy, so never the twain could or should meet. But being a sensible old lady she knew that Catherine Bush was what the thinning Blue Blood of England needed at that time, and so she sets out to educate this clever girl further. And her words that leapt from the page at me were: 'If you wish to become a lady, you must first of all be well read'. And then she told Catherine Bush the book she must get on which to base her education, and that book was *Lord Chesterfield's Letters to his Son*.

Well, I simply flew down to the South Shields library, the first time, I must confess, I had been inside a library, and I took out the first volume of *Lord Chesterfield's Letters to his Son*.

My statement that from this time I entered into a different life is no exaggeration, for this man became my tutor and the Public Library my University. Lord Chesterfield gave me a taste of my first mythology; he led me into real history and geography; he taught me how to read, simply because he knew how to write. There is not one page in one of his four-hundred and seventeen letters to this son from which some piece of knowledge cannot be gleaned. He spoke of writers I had never heard of, and likely would never have heard of but for him: Pope, Voltaire, Dean Swift, on and on.

Remember, I was still working in the workhouse laundry. I was then an assistant manageress, and up to that time I had been driven by an urge I couldn't understand, except that it led me to writing, to the fiddle, to French, and to the muscle-producing Indian clubs; but now I seemed to know where I was going, at least what I wanted to do, if not exactly be: I wanted education because this man, through his letters, had pointed out to me that I was abysmally ignorant. I knew nothing. I had been nowhere. Yet, with the bumptious Northern traits in me I had, up to that time, thought I knew more than most, for wasn't I different? Hadn't I in me qualities of my unknown father whom I understood to have been a gentleman? Just as my almost acute sensivity in my young life had caused me to suffer the indignities of being illegitimate, so I also held pride that I was of a better class than those about me; and this developed while in Harton Institution, for I would prostitute my talent by belittling my intelligence in acting the goat and allowing myself to be the butt for laughter among the eighteen staff with whom I worked and lived. Did I not laugh with them at my attempts . . . at culture? Did I not read to them at meal times my silly rhymes? And all with the desire, inwardly denied, of wanting to be liked, wanting to be accepted. Oh yes, wanting to be accepted. So strong was this desire that I had hidden from them the fact that I read T.P. and Cassell's Weekly and John O'London's, for I felt these would have indicated I was getting above myself, and, after all, what was I? Everyone knew . . . a bastard, and from a drunken family.

But all that was now changed: I had a mentor, a friend; and the fact that I was in the same boat as his son drew me closer to him.

Well now, what did I find in this man that was so different, this man who was changing my life? Straightaway, I discovered he was a teacher, for was not the first letter he wrote to his seven-year-old illegitimate son a lesson? As, indeed, I soon found were all those that followed. I golloped them up page after page. Of course, there were things about him that surprised me. First, he didn't like laughter. Laughter – that is frequent and loud laughter – 'is the characteristic of folly and ill manners'.

Well now, a sense of humour had been my saving grace over the difficult years and, as I have indicated, I was always good for a laugh in the mess room. However, I wanted and was determined to follow Chesterfield to the letter. He would allow a smile, but no laughter. So, what did Katie McMullen do? She did not laugh out loud any more, and the staff, at any rate those at my table, became concerned. They imagined me to be either ill or hiding some trouble, and with this in mind they went to the assistant matron; and later, there I was, standing before her.

'Are you feeling unwell, Miss McMullen?'

'No, Miss Smith.'

'Has . . . has some member of the staff upset you in any way?'

Yes, a number of the staff had upset me in many ways, but I couldn't say this.

'No, Miss Smith.'

'Have you any trouble at home?'

There was always trouble at home, but I stated emphatically, 'No, Miss Smith.'

Then Miss Smith, sitting back in her chair, looked at me and said, 'If that is the case, Miss McMullen, what I think you need is a large dose of opening medicine. Go and see Miss Lodge.'

It was too much. When I got outside the door I spluttered, and later apologised to Lord Chesterfield, telling him I couldn't follow him in this case.

A second thing that surprised me about him was his opinion of women. He thought them, to put it plainly, to be mostly numskulls, they were there mainly for the amusement of the male. Yet he had special friends among them, and made great use of many, and spoke highly of one here and there.

I left the North in 1929, spent nine months in Essex as a head laundress, then in January 1930 I went on to Hastings where I was to carry out this work for the next nine years. Also, I bought a large house which I ran as a Guest House. So life was very full: there was little time for reading; what spare time I had I wrote, and mostly humorous pieces.

Isn't it odd that the clown laughs while his heart breaks. I was in much the same state, for during that period I showed a smiling front while going through a form of mental torment.

Chesterfield's *Letters*, Chesterfield's theories were still with me. I would dip into them now and again. But it wasn't until the war began and I married my Grammar School master and was evacuated to St. Albans that, once more, we became tutor and pupil.

From July 1940 until August 1941, we were fortunate enough to have a little flat in Victoria Street, practically opposite the library; and for the first time in my life I had time to myself: no walking a mile and a half to work and then back at night, winter and summer; no worry of staff and mentally-deficient inmates; no more the added work of an evening seeing to the Guest House; no more the longing to sleep; now, I had time.

Even though I spent some of that time in bed losing a baby, it wasn't wasted. My friend was back; I was going through his letters again. Now, not only was he taking me further into knowledge, but also I was learning more about him. Book after book of his life, I read; and what a life! No wonder he had enthralled me from his first letter. Here was a man, of whom it could be said, he had every quality. Yet I was then asking, why was he disliked so much by the Victorians. From this distance and knowledge, I can see now it was because they were hypocrites. They were blaming a man for writing about his own time, about the requirements needed to live in that time and class. His letters were to enable his son to survive and present himself in that class. Moreover, his letters were unearthing the vices of the day which, up till then, had been the prerogative of the few. I was now reading others' opinions of him; I was learning about his life.

At the same time I made a list of all the books that I should read. Most I enjoyed, although many needed studying rather than just reading, and I must admit there were some I could not get through. I felt I was labouring, as it were, until I decided that was what the authors of these same books were doing, their writing was laboured.

And it is this very fact that brings me to Chesterfield's

writing. He said he wrote plain English, and that's exactly what he did. Every word he wrote spoke its meaning clear, every sentence complete with no hyperbole, nothing wasted, nothing overstated. That I myself write plain English now (perhaps with a Geordie word here and there) is all due to this man. And the more I learned about him the more I became amazed at the extent of his knowledge, his ability, and his charm.

Oh, the latter was a surprise, because when first I started to read his letters I had the picture in my mind of this tall, handsome, vigorous individual. Then I saw a picture of him in his robes. Dear! Dear! Dear! He was undersized; he looked ugly; there was nothing about him to suggest charm. Yet, how was it the women fell over themselves to be with him? I had to learn he was possessed of the Graces and this was due to, I think, his grandmother, Gertrude Pierrepont, the Marchioness of Halifax, because from the age of two he had been brought up by her and she taught him what was called the Graces.

Chesterfield's father, the third Earl of Chesterfield, was a rake, a kind of man who apparently never grew up because he shunned responsibility for both his wife and his family. His wife died when she was thirty-three. She had been married for sixteen years and had borne nine children of whom Philip was the second.

The war years were very traumatic for me. I had my own war – a breakdown – to fight. And when in 1945 I returned to Hastings, my husband still being in the Air Force I lived alone in a large rambling house until he was demobilised in 1946. During this time I had been writing again, mostly plays, à la Lord Chesterfield, but not quite, for they were peopled with the upper middle class, not the aristocracy. But after having written the third play I questioned myself as to what I really knew about the characters of the people of whom I was writing. The answer was nothing. But there was a mass of people crowding my mind that I knew inside out. These were the people I had moved away from, to put it plainly, didn't want any truck with. Yet there they were, dozens of them, hundreds of them, their characteristics shouting at me. But I asked myself: after all the years of study and which sprang from this great man, was I going to use my learning on these common people?

Then the mirror of the breakdown was held up to me and I saw myself as I really was. I was a fugitïve from my ain folk. I had been running away for years. There was a pseudo-lady covering the real me, and I knew if I was ever going to write a word that anybody would want to read, I'd have to strip her off and be myself. And I remembered what Lord Chesterfield had said in his will when leaving each of his servants two years wages, words to the effect: 'These men are my equals in nature, they are my inferiors only in fortune.' I have always considered these were great words from a great man. How many of today's gentry would have the courage to say that?

Anyway, the facade went and I opened the locked doors of my mind and out poured the characters of my people, ones I'd rubbed shoulders with for twenty-three years and whose facet of character I, seemingly unconsciously, had imbibed, for once released they became alive on the page. And following the instructions of my tutor I portrayed them in plain English. Not but that my spelling and grammar was wanting at times; but the story was there and the construction of the story was there, and my thoughts were stripped of ostentation, and I was writing from knowledge. And so, after a number of short stories I wrote my first novel.

This was started in 1947, and it was accepted by the first publisher to whom it was sent, Macdonalds.

I was away.

Now began another side to my life, appearances on platforms and openings: Mother's Meetings, Church Fairs, Townswomen's Guilds, W.I.'s. The requests came pouring in and, like every new author, I obliged them gladly . . . What did I talk about? Not how I wrote my first novel. No; I started at the beginning and talked about the first man in my life, my step-grandfather, a drunken ignorant Irishman who could neither read nor write but who seemed to know from the beginning that I would one day make a name for myself. As he put it: with my imagination I'd end up either in the clink or in the money.

Now John McMullen was a hard-drinking, hard-fighting and swearing man, but there was one good point at least in his make-up, he loved me. So, portraying my life with him from the platform evoked both laughter and tears from my audience.

But as time went on I felt I should add a little culture to my talks, and who better to create this atmosphere than my dear Lord Chesterfield? But it was soon made clear to me that the majority of people weren't out to learn about a great statesman, a great gentleman, a great writer; no, they would apparently rather hear about my life with my granda, and were more than interested and willing to listen to the traumata that one experiences in a breakdown. And this, too, was understandable because, following on the war, there were a great many people suffering from nerves.

This disinclination to learn wasn't because those in my audience were unintelligent, but because they had come there that afternoon or evening to be entertained. This was proved quite definitely one night when, rising to 'talk' to a large audience, there, sitting in the front row were very clearly the two dead pans on whom I had to concentrate.

Now I must do a little explanation here about dead pans. I had no training in public speaking. There were classes for such, and prizes given, but I would have none of them. I had listened to too many stilted sentences, and watched eyes flicking down to notes, or endured the silent lapses while the speaker fumbled with the pages.

So, very early on in this sideline to my career, I determined that I would never use notes. I would do my homework so thoroughly and in such a way that the listeners would imagine it to be coming straight 'off the cuff'.

It's all right to decide on a course, but to carry it out is a different thing altogether. So, before giving any talk whatever and to whomever, there would be long sessions in the bathroom: first, talking to myself in the mirror; then addressing a blank wall until it smiled or laughed or perhaps cried. And then there were the pauses, the correct pauses, which I knew were essential.

Before going on the platform I always had a bout of catarrh. It would practically choke me. This of course, was brought about by nerves; but once I was looking on that mass of faces ... I say mass; I once had an audience of two old girls and three babies, the rest having taken to the fields to get the harvest in before the storm broke. I've also had as many as two thousand. But always, not counting the two old girls and the babies, there would be, among that audience, some dead pan faces. Most could be bright and expectant, but not the unsuccessful writer or the over-zealous religious, who had probably heard I spoke openly about my giving up my religion during my breakdown; or even someone who knew of my past and would be thinking, who does she think she is anyway? There would be reasons for all such expressions.

Well, I learned a trick. I would appear to be talking to the whole audience, but it would be on this particular face or faces that I would concentrate; and once I got a smile out of them, even a slight change of expression, I would know I had my whole audience.

This was difficult in a large hall holding many people, but these faces were very often near the front, and on this particular night I heard my poor Lord Chesterfield's name uttered with disdain and the voice came from one of the two dead pans sitting right in the middle of the front row.

They were County, definitely, and both elderly. He was the Colonel type. He sat stiffly with a walking stick between his knees, his two hands covering the handle. She, too, sat erect, her Henry Heath hat without a tilt to it; her tweed costume remained buttoned, the revers showing her white silk blouse and a small black bow tie . . . definitely, definitely County.

On first sight of them, I knew I'd have my work cut out, and I must admit to feeling nervous at presenting these two with such a common, coarse individual as me granda. But I was on the platform and I had to do my stuff, and during the next twenty minutes or so my two 'opponents' never moved a muscle, not even during the chuckles and bursts of laughter; only in my 'telling silences' did they seem to be in accord with the others. They could have been stuffed, so little motion did they make.

I always started this particular talk by saying, 'There have been three men in my life,' and first, I would give them me granda. Then when I'd finished with him there would come the pause, an elongated one, and on this particular night I said to myself, the next bit will surely be more in their line. So I began as follows:

'I now come to the second man in my life, namely Philip Dormer Stanhope, fourth Earl of Chesterfield, and I would like to tell you how . . .'

I got no further. The sphinx moved, the stick was thumped twice upon the floor, and in no small voice, he called out, 'We don't want to hear about your Lord Chesterfield. Give us more of your granda!'

At this there was a great roar, some voices calling out, 'Yes! Give us the old boy.'

Well, it was a good job I knew quite a bit more about 'me granda'. And that evening's performance proved two things to me: first, you cannot really judge by appearances, or expressions; and secondly, if I meant to get my dear Lord Chesterfield over to my audience then I would have to give up the idea of instructing them.

Without pride, I can say I am a natural story-teller, and so I thought, why shouldn't I put him over like I do my granda. WHAT! Speak of his Lordship in the same way as I do old John? Yes; why not? Chesterfield would have understood –

'Please their eyes and their ears,' he had written, 'and the work is half done.'

Now, I had read a great many books on Lord Chesterfield during the years and generally they all dealt with his political life in much the same way. Some differed with regards to the Madelena Elizabeth Du Bouchet episode, whether Chesterfield brought her over from The Hague to London, or whether she followed him, bringing her child with her. Some writers pad their books with a great many of his letters, some like Roger Coxon, deal with his critics. This book was very enlightening, but the one I enjoyed most was, *The True Chesterfield* by Willard Connely.

Anyway, from my reading I learned about the man who had written marvellous letters which had been the source of bringing life to my mind, and for me it became like a crusade that others should follow in my footsteps: where, in the first place, the duchess in Elinor Glyn's story had brought Chesterfield into my life, and so had brought life to my mind, so I knew that, out there, there must be one person, just one person in my audience who was thirsting for knowledge as I once had, and who as yet had never heard of Chesterfield except as a type of sofa.

So back to the bathroom, looking glass, and the stone wall; but now I was not reviving memories long past that I could, in myself, authenticate, I was aiming to put over in a lighter form the talents and characteristics of a great gentleman.

The pattern went like this.

Following on me granda's escapades and my breakdown, I would take up a stance, as if I had just recalled something, and begin in an off-hand manner: 'Oh . . . about Chesterfield. Well now, there's a story, there's a man . . . but I suppose you know about him already . . .' That was tact with a capital 'T', for I was to learn that many members of the English or the History Schools of Universities had overlooked him.

'I'm not going to keep you much longer but before I go I'll tell you a little about him. You see, his father happened to be the third Earl of Chesterfield, a man who seemed to have had no sense of responsibility at all: as I understand it, he kept many beds warm, only now and again going home to his wife. Her name was Betty, by the way, and she was the daughter of Lord Halifax, the man they called the Black Marquis. She married old Chesterfield when she was seventeen and she had nine bairns to him, and by the time she was thirty-three she had had enough, she died. Now our Lord Chesterfield had been brought up by his granny from he was two years old, and he hadn't seen his mother very often, so he didn't miss her. His granny was a grand dame. She was Gertrude Pierrepont, the Marchioness of Halifax, and the old lady now took his sister and brought her up too. She was indeed a lady of character, and she knew all the Graces, which was very important in those days, that is, to know the Graces, and these she instilled into young Chesterfield. Now that was his attraction. The Graces, you know, is not the same as charm, and he had plenty of that as well; but the Graces in those days meant being able to pass yourself in the company of the great with the manners of the times.

'Now, young Chesterfield stayed with his granny until he was eighteen, when he went up to Cambridge. And oh! he certainly made himself felt there, not academically, you know, no, but with the lasses. He was there, I think around 1712. His College was Trinity Hall. Now he didn't distinguish himself at Cambridge, and I'm surprised at that, and so he came down and went on a Tour, as all gentlemen of that time were encouraged to do. And in France he shone. He actually shone in some of the great Salons and with the great ladies of the day, and by this time he was also a great friend of the Prince of Wales who made him 'Gentleman Of The Bed Chamber'. This would have been round about 1715 I think; and it was about this time he entered the House of Commons as M.P. for St. Germains . . . Oh, and one thing after another follows: He's Captain of the Guard, and then his father dies and so he succeeds him and becomes the fourth Earl of

Chesterfield. Following on this, he was appointed Ambassador to The Hague, and it is this period I want to tell you about, because in a roundabout way this is where I come in . . . Oh aye; or rather, he comes in to my life . . . Chesterfield was always very fond of bairns and he was friendly with a family in The Hague that had quite a few and when he visited them he would have a game with the bairns up in the nursery. Now the bairns had a nursemaid; but she wasn't any common kind of nursemaid, oh no, she was a Huguenot and she had escaped with her people from France in the trouble, and it was a sort of pastime with her, attending to these bairns. Well, after he had bounced the bairns on his knee for a time, I think he must have bounced her an'all (which seemed quite natural for a gentleman to do in those days . . . and they haven't changed much today, have they?) . . .

'Anyway, the result of this was that Madelena Elizabeth Du Bouchet had his baby, and it was about this time that Chesterfield was recalled from The Hague and dismissed his office because he had opposed Mr. Walpole's Excise Bill. About this time, too, his money affairs were in a very poor state for his was a very expensive way of living (he would give dinners and soirees). He had, therefore, to look out for a rich wife. It would seem, however, that they had all been snapped up by this time and the only one left happened to be the King's half-sister, Petronilla Melusina De Schulenberg. Now she was indeed a very rich lady, but the snag was that Chesterfield was wanting a family, a legitimate family, and Melusina was forty years old, so he was taking a long shot, wasn't he? Anyway, he married her. Really it was a queer get-up, for he lived in one house and she next door with her mother; and we are given to understand they got on like a house on fire. But the years were passing. He was now forty-five years old and he had no children. . . But wait, what about his illegitimate son? He had, over the years, provided both for him and the boy's mother – Oh yes, he had done the decent thing by her – but now he decided to educate the lad, and so he engaged a tutor and he sent them off on. . . the Tour.

'And so began *Lord Chesterfield's Letters to his Son.*

'Now, we must not forget that this child was only seven years old when the letters started and the little lad had to answer his father's letters by hand and often in French. Under Chesterfield's direction the tour took in one country after another, and continued on year after year. And of course, all the time Lord Chesterfield, while becoming older and increasingly gouty and deaf, was writing to his son imparting the kind of advice which could never have been derived from a formal education.

'In 1738, this son, who had held diplomatic appointments in Europe, dies. He was thirty-six years old, and with his death, came the revelation that he was married and had two sons. Well! Well! I ask you. What a great shock this must have been to our dear Lord Chesterfield. However, being the man he was, he made suitable provision for his daughter-in-law and his grandsons. But he hadn't long to live himself. In March 1773 he followed his son. And it was written that he was the courteous gentleman up to his last breath, when he ordered a chair to be fetched to his bedside so that a visitor could be seated.'

By this time in my talk I would cease to put over his Lordship in a colloquial way for, with luck I should have caught the interest of my audience, at least I would have hoped so. I would then finish by telling them what the letters had meant to me, and how it pained me that this great man was maligned, a man who had held many positions in the government and who should have been Prime Minister. This man who, first of all, was an educationalist, then an essayist, a diplomat, a historian, a wit, a parliamentarian, but above all, a man who understood humanity. And you know, if I come across anyone who, when in conversation and Chesterfield's name is mentioned, says, 'Oh, Dr. Johnson said of him, "He had the manners of a dancing master and the morals of a whore,"' I know instantly that that person has never read a serious word that Lord Chesterfield had written or that anyone else had written about him. Dr. Johnson's spite was born when Chesterfield did not rush to his assistance when he was compiling his dictionary.

What faults Chesterfield had were mainly those of his time. I think he was not capable of doing a mean action. He knew human nature inside out and he was fearless in speaking the truth. One of his platforms for this was the magazine 'The World', in which he wrote, what he called, plain English, and with this he lashed hypocrisy and cant. Why he was reviled for showing up the foibles of human nature, I shall never know. With regard to the lessons he gave to his son, he was merely instructing him in the matter of perception with regard to the characters of the people of his day, the frivolousness and stupidity of some women, and the duplicity of many men. In short he was preparing him for a life at Court.

Well, it was in this way I got my Lord Chesterfield over to my audiences, and it was always with delight that I would read in a 'fan' letter the fact that the sender had gone to the library and got out *Lord Chesterfield's Letters to his Son*.

What more can I say about my dear Chesterfield? Only that I know that this volume will open up his priceless wisdom to many, and if only to a few it takes on the form of tutor, as his letters did for me, then I can hear him again saying, 'You whom I consider as unfortunate friends, my equals by nature, and my inferiors only by the difference of our fortunes'.

BORN TO SUCCESS?

CHAPTER

1

T the message that rings out from these letters is that success is not a matter of luck, rather the product of an overall strategy, worked at and perfected over time. From the outset, Chesterfield denies the value of high birth, that first lucky roll of the dice. 'If it means anything,' he wrote in 'The World', an 18th-century journal, 'it means a long lineal descent from a founder, whose industry or good fortune, whose merit, or perhaps guilt, has enabled his posterity to live useless to society, and to transmit to theirs their pride and patrimony.' Rather than upholding society, high birth merely seems to lead to a decline: 'I must confess that, before I got the key to this fashionable language, I was a good deal puzzled myself with the distinction between birth and no birth; . . . I foolishly imagined that well-born meant born with a sound mind in a sound body . . . But I never suspected that it could possibly mean the shrivelled tasteless fruit of an old genealogical tree.'

To such a rationalist as Chesterfield, the rewards feted by society upon people for no other reason than a fortuitous birth seemed ludicrous. A more reliable system of merit was required, for 'the truth is that nature, seldom profuse, and seldom niggardly, has distributed her gifts more equally than she is generally supposed to have done. Education and situations make the great difference. Culture improves, and occasions elicit natural talents.'

In the modern context, therefore, Chesterfield belongs to the behaviourist school of psychology, the tenets of which are contained in this well-known quotation from its founder, John B. Watson: 'Give me a dozen healthy infants, well-formed, and my own special world to bring them up in and I will guarantee to take any one at random and train him to become any type of specialist I might select – doctor, lawyer, artist, merchant-chief and, yes, even beggar man and thief, regardless of his talents, penchants, dependencies, abilities, vocation and the race of his ancestors.'

Dear Boy,   *June, 1740*

I write to you now, in the supposition that you continue to deserve my attention as much as you did when I left London, and that Mr. Maittaire would commend you as much now as he did the last time he was with me; for, otherwise, you know very well that I should not concern myself about you. Take care, therefore, that when I come to town I may not find myself mistaken in the good opinion I entertained of you in my absence.

I hope you have got the linnets and bullfinches you so much wanted, and I recommend the bullfinches to your imitation. Bullfinches, you must know, have no natural note of their own, and never sing, unless taught; but will learn tunes better than any other birds. This they do by attention and memory; and you may observe, that, while they are taught, they listen with great care, and never jump about and kick their heels. Now I really think it would be a great shame for you to be outdone by your own bullfinch.

I take it for granted, that, by your late care and attention, you are now perfect in Latin verses, and that you may at present be called, what Horace desired to be called, *Romanæ fidicen Lyræ*. Your Greek too, I dare say, keeps pace with your Latin; and you have all your pardigms *ad ungeum.*

You cannot imagine what alterations and improvements I expect to find every day, now that you are more than *octennis.* And at this age, *non progedi* would be *regredi*, which would be very shameful.

Adieu! Do not write to me; for I shall be in no settled place to receive letters while I am in the country.

Dear Boy,   *October, 1746*

A *propos* of negligence; I must say something to you upon that subject. You know I have often told you, that my affection for you was not a weak womanish one; and, far from blinding me, it makes me but more quick-sighted, as to your faults: those it is not only my right, but my duty, to tell you of; and it is your duty and your interest to correct them. In the strict scrutiny which I

Any man of common understanding may, by proper culture, care, attention, and labour, make himself whatever he pleases, except a good poet.

---

have into you, I have (thank God) hitherto not discovered any vice of the heart, or any peculiar weakness of the head; I have discovered laziness, inattention, and indifference; faults which are only pardonable in old men, who, in the decline of life, when health and spirits fail, have a kind of claim to that sort of tranquillity. But a young man should be ambitious to shine and excel; alert, active, and indefatigable in the means of doing it; and, like Cæsar, *Nil actum reputans, si quid superesset agendum.* You seem to want that *vivida vis animi*, which spurs and excites most young men to please, to shine, to excel. Without the desire and the pains necessary to be considerable, depend upon it, you never can be so; as, without the desire and attention necessary to please, you never can please. *Nullum numen abest, si sit prudentia,* is unquestionably true with regard to everything except poetry; and I am very sure that any man of common understanding may, by proper culture, care, attention and labour, make himself whatever he pleases, except a good poet.

Dear Boy,   *April, 1748*

I have not received any letter, either from you or from Mr. Harte, these three posts, which I impute wholly to accidents between this place and Leipsig; and they are distant enough to admit of many. I always take it for granted that you are well, when I do not hear to the contrary; besides, as I have often told you, I am much more anxious about your doing well, than about your *being* well; and, when you do not write, I will suppose that you are doing something more useful. Your health will continue while your temperance continues; and, at your age, Nature takes sufficient care of the body, provided she is left to herself, and that intemperance on one hand, or medicines on the other, do not break in upon her. But it is by no means so with the mind, which, at your age particularly, requires great and constant care, and some physic. Every quarter of an hour, well or ill employed, will do it essential and lasting good or harm. It requires, also, a great deal of exercise, to bring it to a state of health and vigour.

Observe the difference there is between minds cultivated and minds uncultivated, and you will, I am sure, think you cannot take too much pains, nor employ too much of your time in the culture of your own. A drayman is probably born with as good organs as Milton, Locke, or Newton; but, by culture, they are much more above him than he is above his horse. Sometimes, indeed, extraordinary geniuses have broken out by the force of nature, without the assistance of education; but those instances are too rare for anybody to trust to; and even they would make a much greater figure, if they had the advantage of education into the bargain. If Shakespeare's genius had been cultivated, those beauties, which we so justly admire in him, would have been undisguised by those extravagances and that nonsense with which they are frequently accompanied.

People are, in general, what they are made, by education and company, from fifteen to five-and-twenty; consider well, therefore, the importance of your next eight or nine years—your whole depends upon them.

THE ART OF LEARNING

CHAPTER
2

Chesterfield's earliest demand of Philip was that he should be a scholar. Following the early private tutorials – a Mr. Maittaire was head tutor to the boy, and by the age of six Philip was already learning Latin and French – Chesterfield sent his son to Westminster School, a choice that was not entirely satisfactory, judging by Chesterfield's later description of the place as 'undoubtedly the seat of illiberal manners and brutal behaviour'. Philip spent three or so years at the school (from the age of 11 to 13), between 1743 and 1746.

Behind all Chesterfield's ideas of education lie the ideas of John Locke, father of the empirical school of philosophy. It was his two books *Some Thoughts Concerning Education* and *The Conduct of Understanding* which were of particular interest to Chesterfield, he frequently quoted from them and recommended them to his son. Central to Locke's empirical philosophy was the importance of knowledge acquired from experience as against innate knowledge or intuition. His model of the mind was that of a 'tabula rasa', a white sheet, receptive to impressions. Clearly this corresponds to Chesterfield's system of education. Philip was to be that white sheet, his father's manuscript. Indeed, Chesterfield often indulged in fanciful conceits of his son's progress using just such imagery: 'I hope to be presented every year with a new edition of you, more correct than the former, and considerably enlarged.' Philip was to be shaped much as a work of art, continually polished, edited, re-drawn.

Such deliberate, calculated moulding of the self was typical of the 18th Century, an age which sought to detach itself from the errancies of Nature. As a critic has written, 'Chesterfield is often spoken of as "artifical", and in the broadest sense that he scorned the primitive . . .' (*Coxon*). He lived in a century that imposed order on Nature by classifying the world in dictionaries and encyclopaedias. Samuel Johnson, in the Preface to his dictionary, wrote of the English language like a garden that had 'gone wild' and spread in 'wild exuberance', his job was the 'cultivation of every species of literature'.

Philip, in his schooldays, was to become something of an encyclopaedia, an archive of quotations and excerpts amassed in even the most inopportune moments.

But, above all, Chesterfield was a practical man, and in his treatment of learning there is always a discernible profit motive. For Chesterfield, knowledge operates like a deposit, to be drawn upon at a later time: 'Let me, therefore, most earnestly recommend to you to hoard up, while you can, a great stock of knowledge; for though, during the dissipation of your youth, you may not have occasion to spend much of it, yet, you may depend upon it, that a time will come when you will want it to maintain you.' Ideas, concepts, quotations become valuable property stored in the lumber room of the head. Chesterfield recommends that Philip draw up lists of his reading, a stock list, much as Defoe's Robinson Crusoe makes inventories of his possessions. But always there is the emphasis upon utility, upon knowledge as a good investment. Time spent now acquires greater value later on. This too was symptomatic of Chesterfield's period. The rise of commerce in the 18th Century gave a new value to time since it became commensurate with money. Sales of calendars, diaries and account books rose as people became more concerned with the ephemeral commodity, Time. Newspapers and broadsheets, containing market and political information, led people to look ahead. Coach schedules and the Royal Mail entailed a standardisation of time of day. Chesterfield himself was instrumental in the adoption of the Gregorian calendar.

The profit motive – to get the most out of every hour, every book, every acquaintance – prompts Chesterfield's programme for his son. Knowledge is to be conceived of as a long-term investment. But there is also a hint that learning on its own will not be enough.

Dear Boy,   *December, 1747*
Remember that whatever knowledge you do not solidly lay the foundation of before you are eighteen, you will never be master of while you breathe. Knowledge is a comfortable and necessary retreat and shelter for us in an advanced age; and if we do not plant it while young, it will give us no shade when we grow old. I neither require nor expect from you great application to books after you are once thrown out into the great world. I know it is impossible; and it may even, in some cases, be improper: this, therefore, is your time, and your only time, for unwearied and uninterrupted

If you should sometimes think your application to books a little laborious, consider that labour is the unavoidable fatigue of a necessary journey.

application. If you should sometimes think it a little laborious, consider the labour is the unavoidable fatigue of a necessary journey. The more hours a day you travel,

'The value of moments, when cast up, is immense, if well employed;
if thrown away, their loss is irrecoverable.'

the sooner you will be at your journey's end. The sooner you are qualified for your liberty, the sooner you shall have it; and your manumission will entirely depend upon the manner in which you employ the intermediate time. I think I offer you a very good bargain, when I promise you, upon my word, that, if you will do everything that I would have you do till you are eighteen, I will do everything that you would have me do ever afterwards.

I knew a gentleman, who was so good a manager of time, that he would not even lose that small portion of which the calls of nature obliged him to pass in the necessary-house, but gradually went through all the Latin poets in those moments. He bought, for example, a common edition of Horace, of which he tore off gradually a couple of pages, carried them with him to that necessary place, read them first, and then sent them down as a sacrifice to Cloacina; this was so much time fairly gained; and I recommend to you to follow his example. It is better than only doing what you cannot help doing at those moments; and it will make any book which you shall read in that manner, very present to your mind. Books of science, and of a grave sort, must be read with continuity; but there are very many, and even very useful ones, which may be read with advantage by snatches, and unconnectedly; such are all the good Latin poets, except Virgil in his Æneid: and such are most of the modern poets in which you will find many pieces worth reading that will not take up above seven or eight minutes. Bayle's, Moreri's, and other dictionaries, are proper books to take and shut up for the little intervals of (otherwise) idle time, that everybody has in the course of the day, between either their studies or their pleasures. Good night!

A spirit of rationalism pervaded the 18th Century. Reason was raised to a level of unprecedented importance and created a sense that the errors of previous centuries were now to be dispelled. Vague superstition was to be replaced by scientific truth arrived at by observation, investigation and logical method. Reason is the path to truth. Philip is urged to accept nothing at face value – either the notions of the books that he reads or the apparent virtue of the people he meets. Everything is to be investigated, scrutinised, assessed. Reason, common sense and judgment thus form a vital part of Chesterfield's strategy. Reason becomes a sort of faith, a kind of ultimate arbiter: 'I look upon common sense to be to the mind what conscience is to the heart, the faithful and constant monitor of what is right or wrong. And I am convinced that no man commits either a crime or a folly, but against the manifest and sensible representations of one or the other.'

Use and assert your own reason; reflect, examine, and analyse everything, in order to form a sound and mature judgment.

The relevance today of Chesterfield's call for careful analysis and sound judgment is inescapable. We are daily subjected to a flood of material from newspapers, television, radio, fax, computer, even satellite. As Chesterfield held, information has a real value as a commodity, particularly for its political, commercial and military applications, but its utility depends on judgment. Investment broker or money managers may receive the same information; it is their judgment on it that will make the difference between them. Equally, the constant bombardment of messages to which all of us are exposed through the mass media, require of us an increasingly sophisticated judgmental expertise in order to separate fact from entertaining fiction, or even from deliberate dis-information. Information alone is not enough.

For the majority in Chesterfield's time, 'educational' materials and information sources consisted of a jumbled mass of basic nursery rhymes, spelling books, shop and tavern signs, as well as a sudden proliferation of 'teach yourself' books to supplement an otherwise elitist system of education. With the development of printing processes came the broadsheets, street ballads, and newspapers, and these created our first, mass, 'impulse-buy' reading market and a new incentive to become literate. But the increasing availability of information, and gradual 'democratisation of learning', did little to defeat deep-set prejudice (errant reason), as Chesterfield records:

'My cobbler is also a politician. He reads the first newspaper he can get, desirous to be informed of the state of affairs in Europe, and of the street robberies in London. He has not, I presume, analysed the interests of the respective countries of Europe, nor deeply considered those of his own: still less is he systematically informed of the political duties of a citizen and a subject. But his heart and his habits supply those defects. He glows with zeal for the honour and prosperity of old England, he will fight for it, if there be occasion, and drink to it perhaps a little too often, and too much. However, is it not to be wished that there were in this country six millions of such honest and zealous, though uninformed citizens?

'Our honest cobbler is thoroughly convinced, as his forefathers were for many centuries, that one Englishman can beat three Frenchmen; and, in that persuasion, he would by no means decline the trial. Now, though in my own private opinion, deduced from physical principles, I am apt to believe that one Englishman could beat no more than two Frenchmen of equal strength and size with himself, I should, however, be very unwilling to undeceive him of that useful and sanguine error, which certainly made his countrymen triumph in the fields of Poitiers and Crecy.'

It is a sad comment on our present era, in which publishing and information technology have reached unprecedented levels of growth, and education is available to all, that Chesterfield's cobbler is still very much alive today, though his battleground has shifted to the football terraces of Europe.

Great learning, if not accompanied with sound judgment, frequently carries us into error, pride and pedantry.

Dear Boy,   *February, 1748*

Every excellency, and every virtue, has its kindred vice or weakness; and if carried beyond certain bounds, sinks into the one or the other. Generosity often runs into profusion, economy into avarice, courage into rashness, caution into timidity, and so on; insomuch that, I believe, there is more judgment required for the proper conduct of our virtues, than for avoiding their opposite vices. Vice, in its true light, is so deformed, that it shocks us at first sight; and would hardly ever seduce us, if it did not, at first, wear the mask of some virtue.

But virtue is, in itself, so beautiful, that it charms us at first sight; engages us more and more upon further acquaintance, and, as with other beauties, we think excess impossible, it is here that judgment is necessary, to moderate and direct the effects of an excellent cause.

I shall apply this reasoning at present, not to any particular virtue, but to an excellency, which, for want of judgment, is often the cause of ridiculous and blameable effects; I mean, great learning—which, if not accompanied with sound judgment, frequently carries us into error, pride, and pedantry. As I hope you will possess that excellency in its utmost extent, and yet without its too common failings, the hints, which my experience can suggest, may probably be useless to you.

Some learned men, proud of their knowledge, only speak to decide, and give judgment without appeal. The consequence of which is, that mankind, provoked by the insult and injured by the oppression, revolt; and, in order to shake off the tyranny, even call the lawful authority in question. The more you know, the modester you should be; and (by the bye) that modesty is the surest way of gratifying your vanity. Even where you are sure, seem rather doubtful; represent, but do not pronounce; and, if you would convince others, seem open to conviction yourself.

Others, to show their learning, or often from the prejudices of a school education, where they hear nothing else, are always talking of the ancients as something more than men, and of the moderns as something less. They are never without a classic or two in their pockets; they stick to the old good sense; they read none of the modern trash; and will show you plainly that no improvement has been made, in any one art or science, these last seventeen hundred years. I would by no means have you disown your acquaintance with the ancients, but still less would I have you brag of an exclusive intimacy with them. Speak of the moderns without contempt, and of the ancients without idolatry; judge them all by their merits, but not by their age; and, if you happen to have an Elzevir classic in your pocket, neither show it nor mention it.

Some great scholars, most absurdly, draw all their maxims, both for public and private life, from what they call parallel cases in the ancient authors; without considering that, in the first place, there never were, since the creation of the world, two cases exactly parallel; and, in the next place, that there never was a case stated, or even known, by any historian, with every one of its circumstances; which, however, ought to be known, in order to be reasoned from. Reason upon the case itself, and the several circumstances that attend it, and act accordingly; but not from the authority of ancient poets or historians. Take into your consideration, if you please, cases seemingly analogous; but take them as helps only, not as guides. We are really so prejudiced by our educations, that, as the ancients deified their heroes, we deify their madmen: of which, with all due regard to antiquity, I take Leonidas and Curtius to have been two distinguished ones. And yet a solid pedant would, in a speech in Parliament relative to a tax of twopence in the pound upon some commodity or other, quote those two heroes as examples of what we ought to do and suffer for our country. I have known these absurdities carried so far by people of injudicious learning, that I should not be surprised if some of them were to propose, while we are at war with the Gauls, that a number of geese should be kept in the Tower upon account of the infinite advantage which Rome received, in a *parallel case*, from a certain number of geese in the Capitol. This way of reasoning and this way of speaking will always form a poor politician, and a puerile declaimer.

There is another species of learned men, who, though less dogmatical and supercilious, are not less impertinent. These are the communicative and shining pedants, who adorn their conversation, even with women, by happy quotations of Greek and Latin; and who have contracted such a familiarity with the Greek and Roman authors, that they call them by certain names or epithets denoting intimacy. As *old* Homer; that *sly rogue* Horace; *Maro* instead of Virgil; and *Naso*, instead of Ovid. These are often imitated by coxcombs, who have no learning at all, but who have got some names and some scraps of ancient authors by heart,

Wear your learning, like your watch, in a private pocket; do not pull it out and strike it merely to show you have one.

which they improperly and impertinently retail in all companies, in hopes of passing for scholars. If, therefore, you would avoid the accusation of pedantry on one hand, or the suspicion of ignorance on the other, abstain from learned ostentation. Speak the language of the company that you are in; speak it purely, and unlarded with any other. Never seem wiser, nor more learned, than the people you are with. Wear your learning, like your watch, in a private pocket; and do not pull it out and strike it merely to show you have one. If you are asked what o'clock it is, tell it; but do not proclaim it hourly and unasked like the watchman.

Of all the troubles, do not decline, as many people do, that of thinking.

Dear Boy,   *February, 1749*
  You are now come to an age capable of reflection [Philip is 16], and I hope you will do, what, however, few people at your age do, exert it, for your own sake, in the search of truth and sound knowledge. I will confess (for I am not unwilling to discover my secrets to you) that it is not many years since I have presumed to reflect for myself. Till sixteen or seventeen, I had no reflection; and, for many years after that, I made no use of what I had. I adopted the notions of the books I read, or the company I kept, without examining whether they were just or not; and I rather chose to run the risk of easy error, than to take the time and trouble of investigating truth. Thus, partly from laziness, partly from dissipation, and partly from the *mauvaise honte* of rejecting

'Take nothing for granted . . . but weigh and consider in your own mind the probability of the facts and the justness of the reflections.'

fashionable notions, I was (as I have since found) hurried away by prejudices, instead of being guided by reason; and quietly cherished error, instead of seeking for truth. But since I have taken the trouble of reasoning for myself, and have had the courage to own that I do so, you cannot imagine how much my notions of things are altered, and in how different a light I now see them, from that in which I formerly viewed them through the deceitful medium of prejudice or authority. Nay, I may possibly still retain many errors, which from long habit, have perhaps grown into real opinions; for it is very difficult to distinguish habits, early acquired and long entertained, from the result of our reason and reflection. . .

Use and assert your own reason; reflect, examine, and analyse everything, in order to form a sound and mature judgment; let no σὖτος ἐφα impose upon your conversation, mislead your actions, or dictate your conversation. Be early what, if you are not, you will, when too late, wish you had been. Consult your reason betimes; I do not say that it will always prove an unerring guide, for human reason is not infallible; but it will prove the least erring guide that you can follow. Books and conversation may assist it; but adopt neither blindly and implicitly; try both by that best rule which God has given to direct us—reason.

Of all the troubles, do not decline, as many people do, that of thinking. The herd of mankind can hardly be said to think; their notions are almost all adoptive; and, in general, I believe it is better that it should be so, as such common prejudices contribute more to order and quiet than their own separate reasonings would do, uncultivated and unimproved as they are. We have many of those useful prejudices in this country, which I should be very sorry to see removed. The good Protestant conviction, that the Pope is both Antichrist and the Whore of Babylon, is a more effectual preservative in this country against Popery than all the solid and unanswerable arguments of Chillingworth. The idle story of the Pretender's having been introduced in a warming-pan into the Queen's bed, though as destitute of all probability as of all foundation, has been much more prejudicial to the cause of Jacobitism than all that Mr. Locke and others have written to show the unreasonableness and absurdity of the doctrines of indefeasible hereditary right and unlimited passive obedience. And that silly, sanguine notion, which is firmly entertained here, that one Englishman can beat three Frenchmen, encourages, and has sometimes enabled, one Englishman, in reality, to beat two. . .

Such gross local prejudices prevail with the herd of mankind, and do not impose upon cultivated, informed, and reflecting minds; but then there are notions equally false, though not so glaringly absurd, which are entertained by people of superior and improved understandings, merely for want of the necessary pains to investigate, the proper attention to examine, and the penetration requisite to determine the truth. Those are the prejudices which I would have you guard against by a manly exertion and attention of your reasoning faculty.

MAKE THE WORLD
YOUR SCHOOLROOM

CHAPTER

3

In 1746 Chesterfield decided to remove Philip from Westminster School. Contrary to his own education, Philip was not to go on to Cambridge University. Instead, he was to be sent on a Grand Tour around Europe, like so many young gentlemen of his age. For Chesterfield, learning had its place. It furnishes the foundation on which one builds, but as an end in itself it is inadequate, and at worst collapses into pedantry. The successful man must learn the ways of the world unknown to academia.

The Grand Tour that Philip was to follow differed in an important respect to that of his fellows. Rather than a mere education of taste, which, as Chesterfield suspected, was a vague idea and usually meant spending large quantities of time and money, eating and drinking, Philip's tour was to include intensive tutorials, schooling in etiquette and manners, and introductions to the best society that Europe could provide.

He was to be accompanied by the Reverend Walter Harte, an Oxford academic. It was a peculiar choice considering Chesterfield's increasingly disparaging remarks about the blinkered preoccupations of scholars and the necessity for his son to become a man of the world. As Chesterfield's brother, Sir William Stanhope remarked of Philip's progress: 'What could Chesterfield expect from him? . . . He sent him to Leipsig to learn manners, and that too under the direction of an Oxford pedant!'

The comment ignores the father's personal influence on

the tour, however. Long before Philip had reached the various courts of Europe, Chesterfield had paved the way for him, reviving his old acquaintances, creating favours. At Rome, Philip was introduced to Cardinal Albani, Princess Borghese, the Venetian ambassadress, and the Duc de Nivernais, the ambassador of France. The latter's father had received a present from Chesterfield of an Arab horse, surely guaranteeing Philip a favourable reception. In Paris, Philip was to be guided by Mme. de Monconseil, and Chesterfield had been in lengthy correspondence with her, claiming Philip to be her pupil, her 'galopin', in an attempt to create a real sense of interest in her future charge.

A learned parson, rusting in his cell at Oxford or Cambridge, will reason admirably upon the nature of man . . . and yet, unfortunately, he knows nothing of man, for he has not lived with him.

Dear Boy,   *March, 1751*
    What a happy period of your life is this! Pleasure is now, and ought to be, your business. While you were younger, dry rules, and unconnected words, were the unpleasant objects of your labours. When you grow older, the anxiety, the vexations, the disappointments, inseparable from public business, will require the greatest share of your time and attention; your pleasures may, indeed, conduce to your business, and your

business will quicken your pleasures; but still your time must, at least, be divided; wheareas now it is wholly your own, and cannot be so well employed as in the pleasures of a gentleman. The world is now the only book you want, and almost the only one you ought to read; that necessary book can only be read in company, in public places, at meals, and in *ruelles*. You must be in the pleasures, in order to learn the manners of good company. In premeditated, or in formal business, people conceal, or at least endeavour to conceal, their characters; whereas pleasures discover them, and the heart breaks out through the guard of the understanding. Those are often propitious moments for skilful negotiators to improve.

Let every other book then give way to this great and necessary book, the World; of which there are so many various readings, that it requires a great deal of time and attention to understand it well: contrary to all other books, you must not stay at home, but go abroad to read it; and when you seek it abroad, you will not find it in booksellers' shops and stalls, but in Courts, in *hôtels*, at entertainments, balls, assemblies, spectacles, etc. Put yourself upon the foot of an easy, domestic, but polite familiarity and intimacy, in the several French houses to which you have been introduced. Cultivate them, frequent them, and show a desire of becoming *enfant de la maison*. Get acquainted as much as you can with *les gens de cour*; and observe, carefully, how politely they can differ, and how civilly they can hate; how easy and idle they can seem in the multiplicity of their business; and how they can lay hold of the proper moments to carry it on, in the midst of their pleasures. Courts, alone, teach versatility and politeness; for there is no living there without them.

Dear Boy   *May, 1751*
I would, by all means, have you go now and then, for two or three days, to Maréchal Coigny's, at Orli; it is but a proper civility to that family, which has been particularly civil to you; and, moreover, I would have you familiarise yourself with, and learn the interior and domestic manners of, people of that rank and fashion. I also desire that you will frequent Versailles and St. Cloud, at both which Courts you have been received with distinction. Profit by that distinction, and familiarise yourself at both. Great Courts are the seats of true good-breeding; you are to live at Courts, lose no time in learning them. Go and stay sometimes at Versailles for three or four days, where you will be domestic in the best families, by means of your friend Madame de Puisieux, and mine, L'Abbé de la Ville. Go to the King's and the Dauphin's levées, and distinguish yourself from the rest of your countrymen, who, I dare say, never go there when they can help it. Though the young Frenchmen of fashion may not be worth forming intimate connections with, they are well worth making acquaintance of; and I do not see how you can avoid it, frequenting so many good French houses as you do, where, to be sure, many of them come. . .
When you have got your emaciated Philomath, I desire that his triangles, rhomboids, etc., may not keep you one moment out of the good company you would otherwise be in. Swallow all your learning in the morning, but digest it in company in the evenings. The

reading of ten new characters is more your business now than the reading of twenty odd books; showish and shining people always get the better of all others, though ever so solid.

Dear Boy,   *May, 1753*

I have this day been tired, jaded, nay tormented, by the company of a most worthy, sensible, and learned man, a near relation of mine, who dined and passed the evening with me. This seems a paradox, but is a plain truth; he has no knowledge of the world, no manners, no address; far from talking without book, as is commonly said of people who talk sillily, he only talks by book; which, in general conversation, is ten times worse. He has formed in his own closet, from books, certain systems of everything, argues tenaciously upon those principles, and is both surprised and angry at whatever deviates from them. His theories are good, but unfortunately are all impracticable. Why? Because he has only read and not conversed. He is acquainted with books and an absolute stranger to men. Labouring with his matter, he is delivered of it with pangs; he hesitates, stops in his utterance, and always expresses himself inelegantly. His actions are all ungraceful; so that, with all his merit and knowledge, I would rather converse six hours with the most frivolous tittle-tattle woman, who knew something of the world, than with him.

The preposterous notions of a systematical man, who does not know the world, tire the patience of a man who does. It would be endless to correct his mistakes, nor would he take it kindly; for he has considered everything deliberately, and is very sure that he is in the right.

Impropriety is a characteristic, and a never-failing one, of these people. Regardless, because ignorant, of customs and manners, they violate them every moment. They often shock, though they never mean to offend; never attending either to the general character, or the particular distinguishing circumstances of the people to whom, or before whom, they talk; whereas the knowledge of the world teaches one, that the very same things which are exceedingly right and proper in one company, time, and place, are exceedingly absurd in others. In

A man who has great knowledge from experience and observation . . . is a being as different from and as superior to a man of mere book knowledge, as a well-managed horse is to an ass.

short, a man who has great knowledge from experience and observation, of the characters, customs, and manners of mankind, is a being as different from and as superior to a man of mere book and systematical knowledge, as a well-managed horse is to an ass. Study, therefore, cultivate and frequent men and women; not only in their outward, and consequently guarded, but in their interior, domestic, and consequently less disguised characters and manners.

Adieu!

'A man who has great knowledge from experience and observation, of the characters, customs, and manners of mankind, is a being as

superior to a man of mere book knowledge, as a well-managed horse is to an ass.'

Whilst encouraging the boy to sample the social delights that the tour made available, Chesterfield was alert to the potential dangers lying in wait for his son, how easily a young man could be led astray. With admirable frankness, Chesterfield opened up his past life to his son, advertising his own susceptibilities to temptation, in an effort to save his son a similar fate. Chesterfield could hardly ignore the fact that Philip was himself a living reminder of his own predeliction for the pleasures of the flesh, and while gambling and drinking are censored by Chesterfield, the former was certainly one of his own vices. In the 18th Century as a whole, gambling was rife among the leisured classes, almost a national disease. Gentlemen sat around the card tables at Almack's, Whites and Boodles, and Charles Fox, a notorious gambler, would play for twenty-four hours at a stretch, losing as much as £500 an hour. Heavy drinking was also prevalent among the upper classes, and with the prohibition of French wines, the headier Portuguese port wines encouraged drunkenness.

True to his father's plan, Philip undoubtedly enjoyed the benefits of select company and decorous pleasures during his years abroad. This was confirmed by numerous reports that filtered through to Chesterfield from his many spies spread across Europe. As he wrote: 'I give you fair warning, that at Leipsig I shall have an hundred invisible spies upon you; and shall be exactly informed of everything that you do, and of almost everything that you say. I hope, that, in consequence of those minute informations, I may be able to say of you, what Velleius Paterculus says of Scipio; that, in his whole life, *nihil non laudandum aut dixit, aut fecit, aut sensit*.' Fortunately for Philip, the accounts that Chesterfield received were far from comprehensive. Notably, there was the 'Lausanne episode' of which Chesterfield wasn't to hear until quite some time afterwards. Philip had been joined in Lausanne by a friend, the nineteen-year-old Edward Eliot, son of a rich County family. Together they attended a gathering of local dignitaries, and during the card games in the evening, the boys attached the full-bottomed wigs of the players to their chairs, and snipped their breeches. Going outside they returned to shout 'Fire! Fire!' causing the men to jump to their feet and the inevitable to happen.

Dear Boy,   *March, 1747*

Pleasure is the rock which most young people split upon; they launch out with crowded sails in quest of it, but without a compass to direct their course, or reason sufficient to steer the vessel; for want of which, pain and shame, instead of Pleasure, are the returns of their voyage. Do not think that I mean to snarl at Pleasure, like a Stoic, or to preach against it, like a parson; no, I mean to point it out, and recommend it to you, like an Epicurean; I wish you a great deal; and my only view is to hinder you from mistaking it.

> *If people had no vices but their own, few would have so many as they have.*

The character which most young men first aim at is, that of a Man of Pleasure; but they generally take it upon trust; and, instead of consulting their own taste and inclinations, they blindly adopt whatever those, with whom they chiefly converse, are pleased to call by the name of Pleasure; and a *Man of Pleasure*, in the vulgar acceptation of that phrase, means only a beastly drunkard, an abandoned whoremaster, and a profligate swearer and curser. As it may be of use to you, I am not unwilling, though at the same time ashamed, to own, that the vices of my youth proceeded much more from my silly resolution of being what I heard called a Man of Pleasure, than from my own inclinations. I always naturally hated drinking; and yet I have often drunk, with disgust at the time, attended by great sickness the next day, only because I then considered drinking as a necessary qualification for a fine gentleman, and a Man of Pleasure.

The same as to gaming. I did not want money, and consequently had no occasion to play for it; but I thought Play another necessary ingredient in the composition of a Man of Pleasure, and accordingly I plunged into it without desire, at first; sacrificed a thousand real pleasures to it; and made myself solidly uneasy by it, for thirty the best years of my life.

I was even absurd enough, for a little while, to swear, by way of adorning and completing the shining character which I affected; but this folly I soon laid aside, upon finding both the guilt and the indecency of it.

Thus seduced by fashion, and blindly adopting nominal pleasures, I lost real ones; and my fortune impaired, and my constitution shattered, are, I must confess, the just punishment of my errors.

Take warning then by them; choose your pleasures for yourself, and do not let them be imposed upon you. Follow nature, and not fashion; weigh the present enjoyment of your pleasures against the necessary consequences of them, and then let your own common sense determine your choice.

Dear Boy,   *October, 1747*

People of your age have, commonly, an unguarded frankness about them; which makes them the easy prey and bubbles of the artful and the inexperienced; they look upon every knave, or fool, who tells them that he is their friend, to be really so; and pay that profession of simulated friendship, with an indiscreet and unbounded confidence, always to their loss, often to their ruin. Beware, therefore, now that you are coming into the world, of these proffered friendships. Receive them with great civility, but with great incredulity too; and pay them with compliments, but not with confidence. Do not let your vanity, and self-love, make you suppose that people become your friends at first sight, or even upon a

---

Real friendship is a slow grower; and never thrives, unless ingrafted upon a stock of known and reciprocal merit.

---

short acquaintance. Real friendship is a slow grower; and never thrives, unless ingrafted upon a stock of known and reciprocal merit.

There is another kind of nominal friendship, among young people, which is warm for the time, but, by good luck, of short duration. This friendship is hastily produced, by their being accidentally thrown together, and pursuing the same course of riot and debauchery. A fine friendship, truly! and well cemented by drunken-

'Pleasure – the rock which most young people split upon.'

ness and lewdness. It should rather be called a conspiracy against morals and good manners, and be punished as such by the civil magistrate. However, they have the impudence, and the folly, to call this confederacy a friendship. They lend one another money, for bad purposes; they engage in quarrels, offensive and defensive, for their accomplices; they tell one another all they know, and often more too; when, of a sudden, some accident disperses them, and they think no more of each other, unless it be to betray and laugh at their imprudent confidence. Remember to make a great difference between companions and friends; for a very complaisant and agreeable companion may, and often does, prove a very improper and a very dangerous friend.

People will, in a great degree, and not without reason, form their opinion of you, upon that which they have of your friends; and there is a Spanish proverb, which says very justly, *Tell me whom you live with, and I will tell you who you are.* One may fairly suppose, that a man, who makes a knave or a fool his friend, has something very bad to do or to conceal. But, at the same time that you carefully decline the friendship of knaves and fools, if it can be called friendship, there is no occasion to make either of them your enemies, wantonly, and unprovoked; for they are numerous bodies; and I would rather choose a secure neutrality, than alliance, or war, with either of them. You may be a declared enemy to their vices and follies, without being marked out by them as a personal one. Their enmity is the next dangerous thing to their friendship. Have a real reserve with almost everybody, and have a seeming reserve with almost nobody; for it is very disagreeable to seem reserved, and very dangerous not to be so. Few people find the true medium; many are ridiculously mysterious and reserved upon trifles; and many imprudently communicative of all they know.

Dear Boy,   *October, 1748*

I came here [to Bath] three days ago, upon account of a disorder in my stomach, which affected my head, and gave me vertigos. I already find myself something better; and consequently, do not doubt that a course of these waters will set me quite right. But, however, and wherever I am, your welfare, your character, your knowledge, and your morals, employ my thoughts more than anything that can happen to me, or that I can fear or hope for myself. I am going off the stage, you are coming upon it; with me, what has been, has been, and reflection now would come too late; with you, everything is to come, even, in some manner, reflection itself; so that this is the very time when my reflections, the result of experience, may be of use to you, by supplying the want of yours. As soon as you leave Leipsig, you will gradually be going into the great world; where the first impressions that you shall give of yourself will be of great importance to you; but those which you shall receive will be decisive, for they always stick. To keep good company, especially at your first setting out, is the way to receive good impressions. If you ask me what I mean by good company, I will confess to you, that it is pretty difficult to define; but I will endeavour to make you understand it as well as I can.

Good company is not what respective sets of company are pleased either to call or think themselves, but it is that company which all the people of the place call and acknowledge to be good company, notwithstanding some objections which they may form to some of the individuals who compose it. It consists chiefly (but by no means without exception) of people of considerable birth, rank, and character; for people of neither birth nor rank are frequently, and very justly, admitted into it, if distinguished by any peculiar merit, or eminency in any liberal art or science. Nay, so motley a thing is good company that many people, without birth, rank, or merit, intrude into it by their own forwardness, and others slide into it by the protection of some considerable person; and some even of indifferent characters and morals make part of it. But, in the main, the good part preponderates, and people of infamous and blasted characters are never admitted. In this fashionable good company, the best manners and the best language of the place are most unquestionably to be learnt; for they establish and give the tone to both, which are therefore called the language and manners of good company, there being no legal tribunal to ascertain either.

A company wholly composed of men of learning, though greatly to be valued and respected, is not meant by the words *good company*; they cannot have the easy manners and *tournure* of the world, as they do not live in it. If you can bear your part well in such a company, it is extremely right to be in it sometimes, and you will be but more esteemed in other companies for having a place in that; but then do not let it engross you, for, if you do, you will be only considered as one of the *literati* by profession, which is not the way either to shine or rise in the world.

The company of professed wits and poets is extremely inviting to most young men, who, if they have wit themselves, are pleased with it, and, if they have none, are sillily proud of being one of it; but it should be frequented with moderation and judgment, and you should by no means give yourself up to it. A wit is a very unpopular denomination, as it carries terror along with it; and people in general are as much afraid of a live wit in company as a woman is of a gun, which she thinks may go off of itself, and do her a mischief. Their acquaintance is, however, worth seeking, and their company worth frequenting; but not exclusively of others, nor to such a degree as to be considered only as one of that particular set.

But the company which of all others you should most carefully avoid, is that low company which, in every sense of the word, is low indeed—low in rank, low in parts, low in manners, and low in merit. You will, perhaps, be surprised that I should think it necessary to warn you against such company; but yet I do not think it wholly unnecessary; after the many instances which I have seen of men of sense and rank, discredited, vilified, and undone, by keeping such company.

Attend, Observe, Imitate

I f the 18th Century raised Reason to an unprecedented level of importance, there was always the danger that this could create a world of pure mental speculation, preferring abstract logical cogitation to the unpredictability of everyday life. Swift foresaw the possibility, and his *Gulliver's Travels* took it to a satirical conclusion, to which Chesterfield alludes in his letters.

Dear Boy,   *September, 1749*

You know, by experience, that I grudge no expense in your education, but I will positively not keep you a flapper. You may read, in Dr. Swift, the description of these flappers, and the use they were to your friends the Laputans; whose minds (Gulliver says) are so taken up with intense speculations, that they neither can speak, nor attend to the discourse of others, without being roused by some external action upon the organs of speech and hearing; for which reason, those people who are able to afford it, always keep a flapper in their family, as one of their domestics, nor ever walk about, or make visits, without him. This flapper is likewise employed diligently to attend his master in his walks, and, upon occasion, to give a soft flap upon his eyes; because he is always so wrapped up in cogitation, that he is in manifest danger of falling down every precipice, and bouncing his head against every post, and, in the streets, of jostling others, or being jostled into the kennel himself . . .

I aver that no man is, in any degree, fit for either business or conversation, who cannot, and does not, direct his attention to the present object, be that what it will . . . In short, I gave you fair warning, that when we meet, if you are absent in mind, I will soon be absent in body.

True to empiricism (the doctrine, discussed by John Locke in his *Essay Concerning Human Understanding*, that all knowledge derives from experience), Chesterfield urges interaction with the real world . . . attention, observation, constant vigilance.

Observe, inquire, attend. There is hardly any place, or any company, where you may not gain knowledge.

Dear Boy,   *February, 1748*

Now that you are in a Lutheran country, go to their churches, and observe the manner of their public worship; attend to their ceremonies, and inquire the meaning and intention of every one of them; and, as you will soon understand German well enough, attend to their sermons, and observe their manner of preaching. Inform yourself of their church government – whether it resides in the Sovereign, or in consistories and synods; whence arises the maintenance of their clergy – whether from tithes, as in England, or from voluntary contribu-

'Nothing can be done well without Attention. Observe minutely, wherever you go.'

tions, or from pensions from the state. Do the same thing when you are in Roman Catholic countries; go to their churches, see all their ceremonies, ask the meaning of them, get the terms explained to you – as for instance, Prime, Tierce, Sexte, Nones, Matins, Angelus, High Mass, Vespers, Compline, etc. Inform yourself of their several religious orders, their founders, their rules, their vows, their habits, their revenues, etc.; but when you frequent places of public worship, as I would have you go to all the different ones you meet with, remember that, however erroneous, they are none of them objects of laughter and ridicule. Honest error is to be pitied, not ridiculed. The object of all the public worships in the world is the same; it is that great eternal Being, who created everything. The different manners of worship are by no means subjects of ridicule; each sect thinks its own the best; and I know no infallible judge, in this world, to decide which is the best. Make the same inquiries, wherever you are, concerning the revenues, the military establishment, the trade, the commerce, and the police of every country. And you would do well to keep a blank-paper book, which the Germans call an *album*; and there, instead of desiring, as they do, every fool they meet with to scribble something, write down all these things, as soon as they come to your knowledge from good authorities.

I had almost forgotten one thing, which I would recommend as an object for your curiosity and information, that is, the administration of justice; which, as it is always carried on in open court, you may, and I would have you, go and see it, with attention and inquiry.

I have now but one anxiety left, which is, concerning

you. I would have you be, what I know nobody is, perfect. As that is impossible, I would have you as near perfection as possible. I know nobody in a fairer way towards it than yourself, if you please. Never were so much pains taken for anybody's education as yours, and never had anybody those opportunities of knowledge and improvement which you have had, and still have. I hope, I wish, I doubt, and I fear alternately. This only I am sure of – that you will prove either the greatest pain, or the greatest pleasure, of

Yours.

Chesterfield's was a period of scrutiny. Implicit in the scientific spirit of his Age was a new way of looking at the world. Lenses of all sorts brought the world into focus, telescopes and microscopes magnifying Creation in the name of Inquiry. Everything was to be subjected to analysis, taken apart, above all, looked at. Thus, Linnaeus, the naturalist and founder of modern botany, classified plants according to name – genus, species and variety – discerning similarities where once there had only been differences, and *vice versa*. And in the letters, human behaviour is now open to the same kind of analysis, the salon is turned into a laboratory.

Dear Boy,   *January, 1748*
     I am edified with the allotment of your time at Leipsig; which is so well employed, from morning till night, that a fool would say, you had none left for yourself; whereas, I am sure you have sense enough to know that such a right use of your time is having it all to yourself; nay, it is even more, for it is laying it out to immense interest; which, in a very few years, will amount to a prodigious capital.
     Though twelve of your fourteen *commensaux* may not

be the liveliest people in the world, and may want (as I easily conceive they do) *le ton de la bonne compagnie, et les grâces,* which I wish you, yet pray take care not to express any contempt, or throw out any ridicule, which, I can assure you, is not more contrary to good manners than to good sense: but endeavour rather to get all the good you can out of them; and something or other is to be got out of everybody. They will, at least, improve you in the German language; and, as they come from different countries, you may put them upon subjects concerning which they must necessarily be able to give you some useful information, let them be ever so dull or disagreeable in general: they will know something, at least, of the laws, customs, government, and considerable families of their respective countries; all which are better known than not, and consequently worth inquir-

> *No one body possesses everything, and almost everybody possesses some one thing worthy of imitation . . . Collect those various parts, and make yourself a mosaic of the whole.*

ing into. There is hardly anybody good for every thing, and there is scarcely anybody who is absolutely good for nothing. A good chymist will extract some spirit or other out of every substance; and a man of parts will, by his dexterity and management, elicit something worth knowing out of every being he converses with.

As you have been introduced to the Duchess of Courland, pray go there as often as ever your more necessary occupations will allow you. I am told she is extremely well-bred, and has parts. Now, though I would not recommend to you to go into women's company in search of solid knowledge or judgment, yet it has its use in other respects; for it certainly polishes the manners, and gives *une certaine tournure*, which is very necessary in the course of the world, and which Englishmen have generally less of than any people in the world.

With the individual now a subject of study, the way was opened to 'a curiously self-detached, deliberate, self-critical process of character formation.' (*Coxon*) Its corollary, Chesterfield's recommendation of 'imitation', appears, on the face of it, one of his least attractive ideas, since it undermines the safe line between 'being' and 'seeming', 'truth' and 'deception', and appears to call into question a fundamental individuality, the gift of a Creator. Throughout the centuries, simulators and professed lovers of artifice have been regarded with unease. For example, Max Beerbohm, something of an 18th-century figure himself, created a scandal in late Victorian England with his call to an age of artifice in 'A Defence of Cosmetics'. Nevertheless, all of us, consciously or unconsciously, have adopted other people – parents, teachers, friends – as role models. Psychologists have shown that it is in the nature of a child's development that it role-plays its parent.

Our belief in an irreducible essence, individual to our being, has been eroded by psychoanalysts, sociologists,

'*A man of sense carefully attends to the local manners of the respective places where he is, and takes for his models those whom he*

observes to be at the head of fashion . . . Choose by your ear more than by your eye.'

molecular biologists, and linguists alike. Even our most cherished expressions are words taken from someone else's mouth. Today, the man who loves a woman cannot say, 'I love you madly,' because, 'he knows that she knows (and that she knows that he knows) that these words have already been written by Barbara Cartland. Still, there is a solution. He can say, "As Barbara Cartland would put it, I love you madly." At this point, having avoided false innocence, having said clearly that it is no longer possible to speak innocently, he will nevertheless have said what he wanted to say to the woman,' to quote the semiologist Umberto Eco.

If our language is an assembly of quotations, then why not our thinking processes? And in any case why should we feel suspicious of imitating others? In other cultures, resistance to imitation is not so strong. The *Hagukure*, the code of the Samurai which was revived by Yukio Mishima as relevant to modern day Japanese society, sees it as integral to one's progress; 'One must create in the mind's eye a suitable model for emulation. The way to create such a model is to think who among one's acquaintances knows how to observe etiquette, propriety, and ceremony; who has the most courage; who is the most eloquent; who is morally beyond reproach; who has the most integrity; who can make up his mind quickly in a crisis, and then to imagine a composite of all these people. The result will be an excellent model quite worthy of imitation.'

Given Chesterfield's belief that few are born to success, that 'people are, in general, what they are made, by education and company, from fifteen to twenty-five', the aim of his preparatory strategy must be to absorb so completely images and concepts, that they become what others recognise as the natural 'you'.

Chesterfield advises Philip to choose a model, just as Woody Allen – the man whose one aim in life is to be somebody else – imitates Humphrey Bogart in the film 'Play It Again, Sam'. Crucially, however, Chesterfield is not proposing mimicry, an unthinking, 'whole person' imitation. One has to pick and choose; find the feature which fits, and learn to discriminate sufficiently even to find something of value within the least notable character.

Dear Boy,   *May, 1753*

Take your notions of things as by observation and experience you find they really are, and not as you read that they are or should be; for they never are quite what they should be. For this purpose, do not content yourself with general and common acquaintance; but, wherever you can, establish yourself, with a kind of domestic familiarity, in good houses. For instance, go again to Orli for two or three days, and so at two or three *reprises*. Go and stay two or three days at a time at Versailles, and improve and extend the acquaintance you have there. Be at home at St. Cloud; and whenever any private person of fashion invites you to pass a few days at his country-house, accept of the invitation. This will necessarily give you a versatility of mind, and a facility to adopt various manners and customs; for everybody desires to please those in whose house they are; and people are only to be pleased in their own way. . . Labour this great point, my dear child, indefatigably; attend to the very smallest parts, the minutest graces, the most trifling circumstances, that can possibly concur in forming the shining character of a complete Gentleman, *un galant homme, un homme de cour,* a man of business and pleasure; *estimé des hommes, recherché des femmes, aimé de tout le monde.* In this view, observe the shining part of every man of fashion who is liked and esteemed; attend to, and imitate that particular accomplishment for which you hear him chiefly celebrated and distinguished; then collect those various parts, and make yourself a mosaic of the whole. No one body possesses everything, and almost everybody possesses some one thing worthy of imitation; only choose your models well; and, in order to do so, choose by your ear more than by your eye. The best model is always that which is most universally allowed to be the best, though in strictness it may possibly not be so. We must take most things as they are, we cannot make them what we would, nor often what they should be; and, where moral duties are not concerned, it is more prudent to follow than to attempt to lead.

Adieu!

Dear Boy,   *January, 1750*

I consider the solid part of your little edifice as so near being finished and completed, that my only remaining care is about the embellishments; and that must now be your principal care too. Adorn yourself with all those graces and accomplishments, which, without solidity are frivolous; but without which, solidity is, to a great degree, useless. Take one man, with a very moderate degree of knowledge, but with a pleasing figure, a prepossessing address, graceful in all that he says and does, polite, *liant*, and, in short, adorned with all the lesser talents; and take another man, with sound sense and profound knowledge, but without the above-mentioned advantages; the former will not only get the better of the latter, in every pursuit of every kind, but in truth there will be no sort of competition between them. But can every man acquire these advantages? I say Yes, if he please; supposing he is in a situation, and in circumstances, to frequent good company. Attention, observation, and imitation, will most infallibly do it.

When you see a man, whose first *abord* strikes you, prepossesses you in his favour, and makes you entertain a good opinion of him, you do not know why: analyse that *abord*, and examine, within yourself, the several parts that compose it; and you will generally find it to be the result, the happy assemblage, of modesty unembarrassed, respect without timidity, a genteel, but unaffected attitude of body and limbs, an open, cheerful, but unsmirking countenance, and a dress, by no means negligent, and yet not foppish. Copy him, then, not servilely, but as some of the greatest masters of painting have copied others; insomuch, that their copies have been equal to the originals, both as to beauty and freedom. When you see a man, who is universally allowed to shine as an agreeable well-bred man, and a fine gentleman (as for example, the Duke de Nivernois), attend to him, watch him carefully; observe in what manner he addresses himself to his superiors, how he lives with his equals, and how he treats his inferiors.

Imitate without mimicking him; be his duplicate, but not his ape.

Mind his turn of conversation, in the several situations of morning visits, the table, and the evening amuse-

'Imitate, without mimicking him; be his duplicate, but not his ape.'

ments. Imitate, without mimicking him; and be his duplicate, but not his ape. You will find that he takes care never to say or do anything that can be construed into a slight, or a negligence; or that can, in any degree, mortify people's vanity and self-love; on the contrary, you will perceive that he makes people pleased with him, by making them first pleased with themselves: he shows respect, regard, esteem, and attention, where they are severally proper; he sows them with care, and he reaps them in plenty.

The amiable accomplishments are all to be acquired by use and imitation; for we are, in truth, more than half what we are, by imitation. The great point is, to choose good models, and to study them with care. People insensibly contract, not only the air, the manners, and the vices, of those with whom they commonly converse, but their virtues too, and even their way of thinking. This is so true, that I have known very plain under-standings catch a certain degree of wit, by constantly conversing with those who had a great deal. Persist, therefore, in keeping the best company, and you will insensibly become like them; but if you add attention and observation, you will very soon be one of them. This inevitable contagion of company, shows you the necessity of keeping the best, and avoiding all other; for in every one, something will stick.

STYLE – PLEASING THE
EYES AND THE EARS

CHAPTER
5

In this body of letters, Chesterfield looks more precisely at
what it is in people's behaviour that Philip should analyse
and imitate. In the early letters, delivered while Philip was still
a boy, good breeding (which becomes virtually synonymous
with style) refers in the main to good manners and etiquette,
and elegance.

The 18th Century witnessed the establishment of a
definite code of manners and the conscious cultivation of
elegance. Samuel Johnson's *Dictionary* sought to fix shades of
meaning and create propriety, precisely what was happening
in social intercourse. Just as it was indecorous for a gentleman
to use the second person 'you' to a lady of his acquaintance,
so it was a violation of the social code to use your knife like a
fork. What might seem trivial was in fact extremely important.
Real values attached to the artifice of manners and etiquette,
new rules outmoding old with strong attendant feelings – as
one cultural historian has written, 'a fork is nothing other than
the embodiment of a specific standard of emotions and a
specific level of revulsion.' (*Elias*)

Dear Boy,   *Between 1741 and 1745*
Though I need not tell one of your age, experience,
and knowledge of the world, how necessary good-
breeding is, to recommend one to mankind; yet, as your
various occupations of Greek and cricket, Latin and
pitch-farthing, may possibly divert your attention from

this object, I take the liberty of reminding you of it, and desiring you to be very well-bred at Lord Orrery's. It is good-breeding alone that can prepossess people in your favour at first sight; more time being necessary to discover greater talents. This good-breeding, you know, does not consist in low bows and formal ceremony; but in an easy, civil, and respectful behaviour. You will, therefore, take care to answer with complaisance, when you are spoken to; to place yourself at the lower end of the table, unless bid to go higher; to drink first to the lady of the house, and next to the master; not to eat awkwardly or dirtily; not to sit when others stand; and to do all this with an air of complaisance, and not with a grave, sour look, as if you did it all unwillingly. I do not mean a silly, insipid smile, that fools have when they would be civil; but an air of sensible good-humour. I hardly know anything so difficult to attain, or so necessary to possess, as perfect good-breeding; which is equally inconsistent with a stiff formality, an impertinent forwardness, and an awkward bashfulness. A little ceremony is often necessary; a certain degree of firmness is absolutely so; and an outward modesty is extremely becoming: the knowledge of the world, and your own observations, must, and alone can, tell you the proper quantities of each.

Mr. Fitzgerald was with me yesterday, and commended you much; go on to deserve commendations, and you will certainly meet with them. Adieu.

Chesterfield's troubled relations with Dr. Johnson have been well rehearsed, but it is instructive to see how the great lexicographer, for all his evident intelligence, fell short of

Chesterfield's ideal of elegance. While the latter's covert description of the 'hottentot' Johnson (*February, 1751*) is often felt to be insensitive, Boswell himself recorded the Doctor's grotesque mannerisms at the table: 'He commonly held his head to one side towards his right shoulder, and shook it in a tremulous manner, moving his body backwards and forwards, and rubbing his left knee in the same direction, with the palm of his hand. In the intervals of articulating he made various sounds with his mouth, sometimes as if ruminating. . . Generally, when he had concluded a period, in the course of a dispute, by which time he was a good deal exhausted by violence and vociferation, he used to blow out his breath like a whale.'

Nothing could be less appealing to Chesterfield.

My Dear Friend,   *February, 1751*
   This epigram in Martial:

> *Non amo te, Sabidi, nec possum dicere quare,*
> *Hoc tantum possum dicere, non amo te;*

has puzzled a great many people; who cannot conceive how it is possible not to love anybody, and yet not to know the reason why. I think I conceive Martial's meaning very clearly, though the nature of epigram, which is to be short, would not allow him to explain it more fully; and I take it to be this: "O Sabidis, you are a very worthy deserving man; you have a thousand good qualities, you have a great deal of learning; I esteem, I respect, but for the soul of me I cannot love you, though I cannot particularly say why. You are not amiable; you have not those engaging manners, those pleasing attentions, those graces, and that address, which are absolutely necessary to please, though impossible to

'O Sabidis, you are a very worthy deserving man; you have a thousand good qualities, you have a great deal of learning . . . but upon the whole you are not agreeable.'

define. I cannot say it is this or that particular thing that hinders me from loving you, it is the whole together; and upon the whole you are not agreeable."

How often have I, in the course of my life, found myself in this situation, with regard to many of my acquaintance, whom I have honoured and respected without being able to love? I did not know why, because, when one is young, one does not take the trouble, nor allow oneself the time, to analyse one's sentiments, and to trace them up to their source. But subsequent observations and reflections have taught me why. There is a man, whose moral character, deep learning, and superior parts, I acknowledge, admire, and respect; but whom it is impossible for me to love, that I am almost in a fever whenever I am in his company. His figure (without being deformed) seems made to disgrace or ridicule the common structure of the human body. His legs and arms are never in the position which, according to the situation of his body, they ought to be in; but constantly employed in committing acts of hostility upon the Graces. He throws anywhere, but down his throat, whatever he means to drink; and only mangles what he means to carve. Inattentive to all the regards of social life, he mis-times or mis-places everything. He disputes with heat, and indiscriminately; mindless of the rank, character and situation of the several gradations of familiarity or respect, he is exactly the same to his superiors, his equals, and his inferiors; and therefore, by a necessary consequence, absurd to two of the three. Is it possible to love such a man? No. The utmost I can do for him, is to consider him a respectable Hottentot.

Chesterfield also realised the importance of clothes in a society which placed so much importance upon show. It was of course a century in which gentlemen of leisure had both time and money to indulge their sartorial whims. Not surprisingly the results were often ludicrous, such as the Macaronis of the '60s and '70s, who wore masses of artificial hair, tiny hats, tight clothes, and carried immense, tasselated walking sticks. Like all areas of 18th-century life, the line between decorum and excess was hard to define.

As with other aspects of Chesterfield's system, there is a belief in the importance of externals, while also recognising them as trivial in themselves. Chesterfield is certainly not recommending foppery, nevertheless 'dress is one of the various ingredients that contribute to the art of pleasing. . .' There are clear parallels to be drawn with the 20th Century. As Yukio Mishima writes of modern Japan, there is an obsessive interest in fashion: 'Today, if you go to a jazz coffee-house and speak with teenagers or young people in their twenties, you will find that they talk of absolutely nothing but how to dress smartly and cut a stylish figure . . . I had no sooner seated myself at a table than a youth at the next table began to cross-examine me: "Did you have those shoes made? Where did you have them made? And your cuff-links, where did you buy them?"'

As in the 18th Century, clothes are now an index of fashionable status. Gucci shoes, Lacoste sportswear, Jermyn Street shirts, Paul Smith boxer shorts, tell people something about you. However, as in Chesterfield's day, their significance goes beyond mere fashion. Clothes are a communicator, they help to describe one's image, the context in which one is to be held. Over the past four decades we have been subliminally schooled by the media in a language of communication which largely comprises visual imagery. Clothes have become minor, but nonetheless effective manipulators in the context of communication. When the then Prime Minister Michael Foot turned up at the Cenotaph on Remembrance Day, 1981, dressed in a donkey jacket, the press screamed disrespect. Conversely, Bob Geldof's similarly relaxed appearance reinforces his no-nonsense approach when campaigning for the Third World. In the second example there appears to be harmony between context and person, in the first there was none. Of course Michael Foot's true feelings were not really expressed by his jacket. Chesterfield's point is that we're all in the act together, and if you want a leading role you must rehearse every aspect of your performance perfectly.

Dear Boy,   *November, 1745*

Now that the Christmas breaking-up draws near, I have ordered Mr. Desnoyers to go to you, during that time, to teach you to dance. I desire you will particularly attend to the graceful motion of your arms; which, with the manner of putting on your hat, and giving your hand, is all that a gentleman need attend to. Dancing is in itself a very trifling, silly thing; but it is one of those established follies to which people of sense are sometimes obliged to conform; and then they should be able to do it well. And, though I would not have you a dancer, yet, when you do dance, I would have you dance well, as

Dress is a very foolish thing; and yet it is a very foolish thing for a man not to be well dressed, according to his rank and way of life.

I would have you do everything you do, well.

There is no one thing so trifling, but which (if it is to be done at all) ought to be done well. And I have often told you, that I wished you even played at pitch, and cricket, better than any boy at Westminster. For instance; dress is a very foolish thing; and yet it is a very foolish thing for a man to to be well dressed, according to his rank and way of life; and it is so far from being a disparagement to any man's understanding, that it is rather a proof of it, to be as well dressed as those whom he lives with: the difference in this case, between a man of sense and a fop, is, that the fop values himself upon his dress; and the man of sense laughs at it, at the same time that he knows he must not neglect it: there are a thousand foolish customs of this kind, which, not being criminal, must be complied with, and even cheerfully, by men of sense. Diogenes the Cynic was a wise man for despising them; but a fool for showing it. Be wiser than other people if you can; but do not tell them so.

Dear Boy,   *June, 1751*

I was talking you over the other day with one very much your friend, and who had often been with you, both at Paris and in Italy. Among the innumerable questions which you may be sure I asked him concerning you, I happened to mention your dress (for, to say the truth, it was the only thing of which I thought him a competent judge), upon which he said that you dressed tolerably well at Paris; but that in Italy you dressed so ill, that he used to joke with you upon it, and even to tear your clothes. Now, I must tell you, that at your age it is as ridiculous not to be very well dressed, as at my age it would be if I were to wear a white feather and red-heeled shoes. Dress is one of the various ingredients that contribute to the art of pleasing; it pleases the eyes at least, and more especially of women. Address yourself to the senses if you would please; dazzle the eyes, soothe and flatter the ears of mankind; engage their heart, and let their reason do its worst against you. *Suaviter in modo* is the great secret. Whenever you find yourself engaged insensibly in favour of anybody of no superior merit or distinguished talent, examine and see what it is that has made those impressions upon you: you will find it to be that *doucer*, that gentleness of manners, that air and address, which I have so often recommended to you; and from thence draw this obvious conclusion, that what pleases you in them will please others in you; for we are all made of the same clay, though some of the lumps are a little finer, and some a little coarser; but, in general, the surest way to judge of others is to examine and analyse one's self thoroughly.

Strict codes of behaviour led, inevitably, to a heightened sense of embarrassment at their transgression, and the period saw a gradual redefinition of distance between people. The individual became aware of himself as separate to others. A need for privacy also became apparent, certain activities should not be seen.

Bodily disgust was never far from the 18th-century mind, the knowledge that man was but an intestinal canal with an orifice at both ends simply overwhelmed the sovereignty of Reason, and the body was seen in its mortal, imperfect state. It is not surprising, then, that Chesterfield should also censure laughter – the uncontrollable rictus of the mouth. For all the nobility of his mind, perhaps man was, after all, nothing more than a machine, an organism prone to sudden spasms and contractions.

That such obsessional attitudes should exist among the elite of society is less surprising in the context of what was largely a grubby, fetid period. Most people took baths rarely, and before cottons became cheap, clothes were difficult to wash. Streets, corridors and stairways were all potential lavatories, and in some dining rooms chamber pots were provided in sideboards so as not to interrupt the flow of conversation. Chesterfield is clearly representative of a more discriminating attitude towards personal hygiene. Examples of physical repulsiveness are rife through the literature of the period, but perhaps none more revealing of the proximity of beauty and repulsiveness than Swift's poems, where the fashionable young damsel is seen as a grotesque puppet, an assemblage of articial props and plasters. As Strephon finds, venturing into 'The Lady's Dressing Room':

The various combs for various uses,
Filled up with dirt so closely fixed,
No brush could force a way betwixt;
A paste of composition rare,
Sweat, dandruff, powder, lead and hair,
A forehead cloth with oil upon't
To smooth the wrinkles on her front;
Here alum flower to stop the steams,
Exhaled from sour unsavoury streams; . . .

Dear Boy,   *July, 1749*

A thorough cleanliness in your person is as necessary for your own health, as it is not to be offensive to other people. Washing yourself, and rubbing your body and limbs frequently with a flesh-brush, will conduce as much to health as to cleanliness. A particular attention to the cleanliness of your mouth, teeth, hands, and nails, is but common decency, in order not to offend people's eyes and noses. Adieu

Dear Boy,   *November, 1750*

You will possibly think that this letter turns upon strange, little trifling objects; and you will think right, if you consider them separately; but if you take them aggregately, you will be convinced that, as parts, which conspire to form that whole, called the exterior of a man of fashion, they are of importance. I shall not dwell now upon those personal graces, that liberal air, and that engaging address, which I have so often recommended to you; but descend still lower—to your dress, cleanliness, and care of your person.

When you come to Paris, you must take care to be extremely well dressed, that is, as the fashionable people are. This does by no means consist in the finery, but in the taste, fitness, and manner of wearing your clothes; a fine suit ill-made, and slatternly or stiffly worn, far from adorning, only exposes the awkwardness of the wearer. Get the best French tailor to make your clothes, whatever they are, in the fashion, and to fit you, and then wear them; button them or unbutton them, as the genteelest people you see do. Let your man learn of the best *friseur* to do your hair well, for that is a very material part of your dress. Take care to have your stockings well gartered up, and your shoes well buckled; for nothing gives a more slovenly air to a man than ill-dressed legs.

In your person you must be accurately clean; and your teeth, hands, and nails should be superlatively so. A dirty mouth has real ill consequences to the owner, for it infallibly causes the decay, as well as the intolerable pain of the teeth; and it is very offensive to his acquaintance, for it will most inevitably stink. I insist therefore that you wash your teeth the first thing that you do every morning, with a soft sponge and warm water, for four or five minutes, and then wash your mouth five or six times. Mouton, whom I desire you will send for upon your arrival at Paris, will give you an opiate, and a liquor to be used sometimes. Nothing looks more ordinary, vulgar, and illiberal, than dirty hands, and ugly, uneven and ragged nails. I do not suspect you of that shocking, awkward trick of biting yours; but that is not enough; you must keep the ends of them smooth and clean—not tipped with black, as the ordinary people's always are. The ends of your nails should be small segments of circles, which, by a very little care in the cutting, they are very easily brought to; every time that you wipe your hands, rub the skin round your nails backwards, that it may not grow up and shorten your nails too much. The cleanliness of the rest of your person, which by the way will conduce greatly to your health, I refer from time to time to the bagnio. My mentioning these particulars arises (I freely own) from some suspicion that the hints are not unnecessary; for when you were a schoolboy, you were slovenly and dirty above your fellows. I must add another caution, which is, that upon no account whatever you put your fingers, as too many people are apt to do, in your nose or ears. It is the most shocking, nasty, vulgar rudeness that can be offered to company; it disgusts one, it turns one's stomach; and, for my own part, I would much rather known that a man's fingers were actually in his breech, than see them in his nose. Wash your ears well every morning, and blow your nose in your handkerchief whenever you have occasion; but, by the way, without looking at it afterwards.

Dear Boy,   *March, 1748*

Having mentioned laughing, I must particularly warn you against it: and I could heartily wish that you may often be seen to smile, but never heard to laugh while you live. Frequent and loud laughter is the characteristic of folly and ill manners: it is the manner in which the mob express their silly joy at silly things; and they call it being merry. In my mind there is nothing so illiberal, and so ill-bred, as audible laughter. True wit, or sense, never yet made anybody laugh; they are above it: they please the mind, and give a cheerfulness to the countenance. But it is low buffoonery, or silly accidents, that always excite laughter; and that is what people of sense and breeding should show themselves above. A man's going to sit down, in the supposition that he had a chair behind him, and falling down upon his breech for want of one, sets a whole company a laughing, when all the wit in the world would not do it; a plain proof, in my mind, how low and unbecoming a thing laughter is. Not to mention the disagreeable noise that it makes, and the shocking distortion of the face that it occasions. Laughter is easily restrained by a very little reflection; but, as it is generally connected with the idea of gaiety, people do not enough attend to its absurdity. I am neither of a melancholy, nor a cynical disposition; and am as willing, and as apt, to be pleased as anybody; but I am sure that, since I have had the full use of my reason, nobody has ever heard me laugh. Many people, at first from awkwardness and *mauvaise honte*, have got a very disagreeable and silly trick of laughing whenever they speak: and I know a man of very good parts, Mr. Waller, who cannot say the commonest thing without laughing; which makes those, who do not know him, take him at first for a natural fool.

Style, or 'good-breeding' as Lord Chesterfield called it – a conglomeration of 'the Graces', les bienséances, or les manières nobles – lies at the heart of Chesterfield's system. Etiquette, social skills, an easy manner, a good appearance, a certain poise, may be external accomplishments, but for Chesterfield they are what count most. They open people's hearts to you, they dispose them favourably to your ideas, they smooth over problems. Style 'cannot be exactly defined, as it consists in a fitness, a propriety of words, actions, and even looks, adapted to the infinite variety and combinations of persons, places, and things. It is a mode, not a substance. . .' (*Essays*)

The 18th Century, an age of rational discourse, is characterised by its sociability, the art of conversation and the hours spent by wits in the London coffee houses. Success in such a society meant the ability to mix well. It was a face-to-face society that thrived on personal connections. As a historian has noted, 'How one made out depended on skills in the games of deference and condescension, patronage and favour, protection and obedience, seizing the breaks and making the most of them. He who did not take his chances was lost.' (*Porter*)

One purpose of 'good-breeding' is, therefore, to oil the wheels of social intercourse: 'Knowledge will introduce him, and good-breeding will endear him to the best companies . . . The scholar, without good-breeding, is a pedant; the philosopher, a cynic; the soldier, a brute; and every man disagreeable.' Philip, the up-and-coming politician and diplomat, must learn that 'the way to the heart is through the senses; please their eyes and their ears, and the work is half done...'

Having himself seen to Philip's introduction to the courts of Europe where he could begin to set up contacts which would serve him in his career, Chesterfield now sets out to discipline him in the social graces that will endear him to

---

We are so made, we love to be pleased better than to be informed . . . Take my word for it, that success depends much more upon manner than matter.

---

them. There is nothing unique to the 18th Century about the idea of practising the art of social skills, as the 20th-century American humourist P J O'Rourke shows in writing that 'conversation is a group activity, and the participants should be thought of as a team, albeit with certain stars. The best teamwork is the result of practice. The best guests for good conversation are guests who've had good conversation with each other before. Their moves are polished. Mr X will give lavish praise to some item of popular culture and pass the ball to Miss Y, who will say something pert.'

In the 18th Century, Swift took a particularly dim view of the elevation of social acrobatics above merit as qualities for advancement at court, and satirised them in the Lilliput section of *Gulliver's Travels*: 'The emperor holds a stick in his hands, both ends parallel to the horizon, while the candidates, advancing one by one, sometimes leap over the stick, sometimes creep under it backwards and forwards several times, according as the stick is advanced or depressed . . .

Whoever performs his part with most agility, and holds out the longest in leaping and creeping, is rewarded with the blue-coloured silk.'

But Chesterfield does not advocate such contorted sycophancy. On the contrary, to so trade one's dignity is self-defeating. While egoism – concern for one's own interests – is paramount in his strategy, egotism – demonstrating an inflated sense of one's own superiority – is specifically discounted. Instead, the model is one of coolly detached poise:

Dear Boy,   *November, 1748*

Of all the men that ever I knew in my life (and I knew him extremely well), the late Duke of Marlborough possessed the Graces in the highest degree, not to say engrossed them; and, indeed, he got the most by them, for I will venture (contrary to the custom of profound historians, who always assign deep causes for great events) to ascribe the better half of the Duke of Marlborough's greatness and riches to those Graces. He was eminently illiterate; wrote bad English, and spelled it still worse. He had no share of what is commonly called *parts*; that is, he had no brightness, nothing shining in his genius. He had, most undoubtedly, an excellent good plain understanding, with sound judgment. But these alone would probably have raised him but something higher than they found him, which was page to King James the Second's Queen. There the Graces protected and promoted him; for, while he was an Ensign of the Guards, the Duchess of Cleveland, then favourite mistress to King Charles the Second, struck by those very Graces, gave him five thousand pounds, with which he immediately bought an annuity

'He could refuse more gracefully than other people could grant; and those who went away from him the most dissatisfied as to the

substance of their business were yet personally charmed and comforted by his manner.'

for his life, of five hundred pounds a year, of my grandfather, Halifax, which was the foundation of his subsequent fortune. His figure was beautiful, but his manner was irresistible, by either man or woman. It was by this engaging, graceful manner, that he was enabled, during all his war, to connect the various and jarring powers of the Grand Alliance, and to carry them on to the main object of the war, notwithstanding their private and separate views, jealousies and wrongheadednesses. Whatever Court he went to (and he was often obliged to go himself to some resty and refractory ones), he as constantly prevailed, and brought them into his measures. The Pensionary Heinsius, a venerable old minister, grown grey in business, and who had governed the republic of the United Provinces for more than forty years, was absolutely governed by the Duke of Marlborough, as that republic feels to this day. He was always cool, and nobody ever observed the least variation in his countenance; he could refuse more gracefully than other people could grant; and those who went away from him the most dissatisfied as to the substance of their business, were yet personally charmed with him and, in some degree, comforted by his manner. With all his gentleness and gracefulness, no man living was more conscious of his situation, nor maintained his dignity better.

In the 18th Century, as today, there is no one particular style that will lead to success. In his *Essays*, Chesterfield is at pains to point to the different requirements of style in different contexts – 'What is good-breeding at St James' would pass for foppery or banter in a remote village; and the homespun civility of that village, would be considered as brutality at court'.

Again it is consistent with his disavowal of whole-person role-playing that he does not advise Philip to mimic the successful style of a particular person. In the end, a successful style is a coming together of all kinds of elements – thoughts, actions, physical appearance, words – which form a pattern that is sound at a given moment, in a given context.

The graces are inherent to the process of self refinement. It is not incidental that Chesterfield compares his son to gold and diamonds, precious minerals which require purifying and polishing before fully realising their value. Character is seen in terms of merchandise, and betrays how inextricable Chesterfield considered 'being' and 'business'.

Dear Boy,   *November, 1750*

There should be in the least, as well as in the greatest parts of a gentleman, *les manières nobles*. Sense will teach you some, observation others; attend carefully to the manners, the diction, the motions, of the people of the first fashion, and form your own upon them. On the other hand, observe a little those of the vulgar, in order to avoid them; for though the things which they say or do may be the same, the manner is always totally different; and in that, and nothing else, consists the characteristic of a man of fashion. The lowest peasant speaks, moves, dresses, eats, and drinks, as much as a man of the first fashion; but does them all quite differently; so that by doing and saying most things in a manner opposite to that of the vulgar, you have a great chance of doing and saying them right.

Dear Boy,   *June, 1748*

Men, as well as women, are much oftener led by their

*Men, as well as women,
are much oftener led by their hearts
than by their understandings. The
way to the heart is through the senses;
please their eyes and their ears, and
the work is half done.*

hearts than by their understandings. The way to the heart is through the senses; please their eyes and their ears, and the work is half done. I have frequently known a man's fortune decided for ever by his first address. If it is pleasing, people are hurried involuntarily into a persuasion that he has a merit which possibly he has not; as, on the other hand, if it is ungraceful, they are immediately prejudiced against him, and unwilling to allow him the merit which it may be he has. Nor is this sentiment so unjust and unreasonable as at first it may seem; for, if a man has parts, he must know of what infinite consequence it is to him to have a graceful manner of speaking, and a genteel and pleasing address: he will cultivate and improve them to the utmost. Your figure is a good one; you have no natural defect in the organs of speech; your address may be engaging and your manner of speaking graceful if you will; so that if they are not so, neither I nor the world can ascribe it to anything but your want of parts.

Dear Boy,

Great talents and great virtues (if you should have them) will procure you the respect and the admiration of mankind; but it is the lesser talents, the *leniores virtutes*, which must procure you their love and affection. The former, unassisted and unadorned by the latter, will extort praise; but will at the same time excite both fear and envy; two sentiments absolutely incompatible with love and affection.

Cæsar had all the great vices, and Cato all the great virtues that men could have. But Cæsar had the *leniores virtutes* which Cato wanted; and which made him beloved even by his enemies, and gained him the hearts of mankind in spite of their reason; while Cato was not even beloved by his friends, notwithstanding the esteem and respect which they could not refuse to his virtues; and I am apt to think that if Cæsar had wanted, and Cato possessed, those *leniores virtutes*, the former would not have attempted (at least with success), and the latter could have protected, the liberties of Rome. Mr. Addison, in his *Cato*, says of Cæsar (and I believe with truth):

Curse on his virtues, they've undone his country.

By which he means those lesser but engaging virtues of gentleness, affability, complaisance, and good-humour. The knowledge of a scholar, the courage of a hero, and the virtue of a Stoic, will be admired; but if the knowledge be accompanied with arrogance, the courage with ferocity, and the virtue with inflexible severity, the man will never be loved. The heroism of Charles XII of

Sweden (if his brutal courage deserves that name) was universally admired, but the man nowhere beloved. Whereas Henry IV of France, who had full as much courage, and was much longer engaged in wars, was generally beloved upon account of his lesser and social virtues. We are all so formed, that our understandings are generally the dupes of our hearts, that is, of our passions; and the surest way to the former is through the latter, which must be engaged by the *leniores virtutes* alone, and the manner of exerting them. . . Everbody feels the impression which an engaging address, an agreeable manner of speaking, and an easy politeness, makes upon them; and they prepare the way for the favourable reception of their betters. Adieu!

Dear Boy,   *November, 1749*
There is natural good-breeding which occurs to every man of common sense, and is practised by every man of common good-nature. This good-breeding is general, independent of modes, and consists in endeavours to please and oblige our fellow-creatures by all good offices short of moral duties. This will be practised by a good-natured American savage as essentially as by the best bred European. But, then, I do not take it to extend to the sacrifice of our own conveniences for the sake of other people's. Utility introduced this sort of good-breeding as it introduced commerce, and established a truck of the little *agrémens* and pleasures of life. I sacrifice such a conveniency to you, you sacrifice another to me; this commerce circulates, and every individual finds his account in it upon the whole. The third sort of good-breeding is local, and is variously

modified, in not only different countries, but in different towns of the same country. But it must be founded upon the two former sorts: they are the matter to which, in this case, fashion and custom only give the different shapes and impressions. Whoever has the two first sorts will easily acquire this third sort of good-breeding, which depends singly upon attention and observation. It is, properly, the polish, the lustre, the last finishing strokes of good-breeding. It is to be found only in capitals, and even there it varies; the good-breeding of Rome differing in some things from that of Paris; that of Paris, in others, from that of Madrid; and that of Madrid, in many things from that of London.

Dear Boy,   *July, 1749*

As I am now no longer in pain about your health, which I trust is perfectly restored, and as, by the various accounts I have had of you, I need not be in pain about your learning, our correspondence may for the future turn upon less important points, comparatively, though still very important ones; I mean, the knowledge of the world, decorum, manners, address, and all those (commonly called little) accomplishments, which are absolutely necessary to give greater accomplishments their full value and lustre.

Had I the admirable ring of Gyges, which rendered the wearer invisible; and had I, at the same time, those magic powers, which were very common formerly, but are now very scarce, of transporting myself by a wish to any given place; my first expedition would be to Venice, there to *reconnoitre* you unseen myself. I would first take you in the morning at breakfast with Mr. Harte, and attend to your natural and unguarded conversation with him; from whence I think I could pretty well judge of your natural turn of mind. How I should rejoice if I overheard you asking him pertinent questions upon useful subjects, or making judicious reflections upon the studies of that morning or the occurrences of the former day! Then I would follow you into the different companies of the day, and carefully observe in what manner you presented yourself to, and behaved yourself with, men of sense and dignity: whether your address was respectful and yet easy, your air modest and yet unembarrassed: and I would at the same time penetrate into their thoughts, in order to know whether your first *abord* made that advantageous impression upon their fancies, which a certain address, air, and manners never fail doing. I would afterwards follow you to the mixed companies of the evening, such as assemblies, suppers, etc., and there watch if you trifled gracefully and genteelly; if your good-breeding and politeness made way for your parts and knowledge.

A diamond, while rough, has indeed its intrinsic value; but till polished, is of no use, and would never be sought or worn.

There is a certain concurrence of various little circumstances which compose what the French call *l'aimable*, and which, now you are entering into the world, you ought to make it your particular study to acquire. Without them, your learning will be pedantry; your conversation often improper—always unpleasant; and your figure, however good in itself, awkward and unengaging. A diamond, while rough, has indeed its intrinsic value; but, till polished, is of no use, and would neither be sought for nor worn. Its great lustre, it is true, proceeds from its solidity and strong cohesion of parts; but, without the last polish, it would remain for ever a dirty rough mineral, in the cabinets of some few curious collectors. You have, I hope, that solidity and cohesion of parts; take now as much pains to get the lustre. Good company, if you make the right use of it, will cut you into shape, and give you the true brilliant polish.

Dear Boy,   *October, 1748*

Having, in my last, pointed out what sort of company you should keep, I will now give you some rules for your conduct in it; rules which my own experience and observation enable me to lay down and communicate to you with some degree of confidence. I have often given you hints of this kind before, but then it has been by snatches; I will now be more regular and methodical. I shall say nothing with regard to your bodily carriage and address, but leave them to the care of your dancing-master, and to your own attention to the best models; remember, however, that they are of consequence.

Talk often, but never long; in that case, if you do not please, at least you are sure not to tire your hearers. Pay your own reckoning, but do not treat the whole company; this being one of the very few cases in which people do not care to be treated, every one being fully convinced that he has wherewithal to pay.

Tell stories very seldom, and absolutely never but where they are very apt, and very short. Omit every circumstance that is not material, and beware of digressions. To have frequent recourse to narrative betrays great want of imagination.

Never hold anybody by the button, or the hand, in order to be heard out; for, if people are not willing to hear you, you had much better hold your tongue than them.

Most long talkers single out some one unfortunate man in company (commonly him whom they observe to be the most silent, or their next neighbour) to whisper, or at least, in a half voice, to convey a continuity of words to. This is excessively ill-bred, and, in some degree, a fraud; conversation-stock being a joint and common property. But, on the other hand, if one of these unmerciful talkers lays hold of you, hear him with patience, and at least seeming attention, if he is worth obliging; for nothing will oblige him more than a patient hearing, as nothing would hurt him more than either to leave him in the midst of his discourse, or to discover your impatience under you affliction.

Take, rather than give, the tone of the company you are in. If you have parts, you will show them, more or less, upon every subject; and, if you have not, you had better talk sillily upon a subject of other people's than of your own choosing.

Avoid as much as you can, in mixed companies, argumentative polemical conversations; which, though they should not, yet certainly do, indispose, for a time, the contending parties towards each other; and, if the controversy grows warm and noisy, endeavour to put an end to it by some genteel levity or joke. I quieted such a conversation hubbub once, by representing to them that, though I was persuaded none there present would repeat, out of company, what passed in it, yet I could not answer for the discretion of the passengers in the street, who must necessarily hear all that was said.

Above all things, and upon all occasions, avoid speaking of yourself, it if be possible. Such is the natural pride and vanity of our hearts, that it perpetually breaks out, even in people of the best parts, in all the various modes and figures of the egotism.

Dear Boy,   *June, 1751*

Les bienséances are a most necessary part of the knowledge of the world. They consist in the relations of persons, things, time, and place; good sense points them out, good company perfects them (supposing always an attention and a desire to please), and good policy recommends them.

Were you to converse with a king, you ought to be as easy and unembarrassed as with your own valet-de-chambre; but yet every look, word, and action, should imply the utmost respect. What would be proper and well-bred with others, much your superiors, would be absurd and ill-bred with one so very much so. You must wait till you are spoken to; you must receive, not give, the subject of conversation; and you must ever take care that the given subject of such conversation does not lead you into any impropriety. The art would be to carry it, if possible, to some indirect flattery; such as commending those virtues in some other person, in which that Prince

'Talk often, but never long; in that case, if you do not please, at least
you are sure not to tire your hearers.'

either thinks he does, or at least would be thought by others to excel.

Almost the same precautions are necessary to be used with ministers, generals, etc. who expect to be treated with very near the same respect as their masters, and commonly deserve it better. There is, however, this difference, that one may begin the conversation with them, if on their side it should happen to drop, provided one does not carry it to any subject, upon which it is improper either for them to speak or be spoken to. In these two cases, certain attitudes and actions would be extremely absurd, because too easy, and consequently disrespectful. As for instance, if you were to put your arms across in your bosom, twirl your snuff-box, trample with your feet, scratch your head, etc., it would be shockingly ill-bred in that company; and, indeed, not extremely well-bred in any other. The great difficulty in those cases, though a very surmountable one by attention and custom, is to join perfect inward ease with perfect outward respect.

In mixed companies with your equals (for in mixed companies all people are to a certain degree equal) greater ease and liberty are allowed; but they too have their bounds within *bienséance*. There is a social respect necessary; you may start your own subject of conversation with modesty, taking great care, however, *de ne jamais parler de cordes dans la maison d'un pendu*. Your words, gestures, and attitudes, have a greater degree of latitude, though by no means an unbounded one. You may have your hands in your pockets, take snuff, sit, stand, or occasionally walk, as you like; but I believe you would not think it very *bienséant* to whistle, put on your

Modes and manners vary in different places and at different times; you must keep pace with them, know them, and adopt them, wherever you find them.

hat, loosen your garters or your buckles, lie down upon a couch, or go to bed and welter in an easy chair. These are negligences and freedoms which one can only take when quite alone; they are injurious to superiors, shocking and offensive to equals, brutal and insulting to inferiors. That easiness of carriage and behaviour, which is exceedingly engaging, widely differs from negligence and inattention, and by no means implies that one may do whatever one pleases; it only means that one is not to be stiff, formal, embarrassed, disconcerted, and ashamed, like country bumpkins, and people who have never been in good company; but it requires great attention to, and a scrupulous observation of *les bienséances*; whatever one ought to do, is to be done with ease and unconcern; whatever is improper must not be done at all.

MAKING FRIENDS
AND INFLUENCING PEOPLE

CHAPTER

6

'Your profession throws you into all the intrigues, and cabals, as well as pleasures, of Courts; in those windings and labyrinths, a knowledge of the world, a discernment of characters, a suppleness and versatility of mind, and an elegancy of manners must be your clue; you must know how to soothe and lull the monsters that guard, and how to address and gain the fair that keep, the golden fleece.'

In politics and business, good connections are as vital to success as they were in 18th-century society. In order to influence a person so as to engage their support, Chesterfield urges Philip to discover their predominant excellency or prevailing weakness, play on either – flatter the first or fulfil the needs created by the second – his letters show how.

Chesterfield has caused a furore among his critics by his analysis of what he regarded to be a common weakness in women, namely vanity, and by his description of the role that women played in the politics of the 18th-century power game. As Churton Collins wrote: 'The contempt with which he speaks of women, and of the relation of women to life, has always appeared to us not merely the one great flaw in his writings, but indicative of the one unsound place in his judgment and temper.' However, he goes on to say, 'The truth is, as it is only just to him to say, that he was generalising from his experience of women of fashion.' And really this is the only justification. As with all aspects of 18th-century society, Chesterfield analysed its machinery, the way power was conducted, how advantage could be gained. How, within any social group, certain people become established as focal figures in the pecking order of power, and as such could be useful to one's cause. Society women, he saw, were in a unique position to make or ruin a man's reputation.

Chesterfield's judgment of women may have been influenced by a particular experience. Early in his career he was Gentleman of the Bed Chamber to the Prince of Wales, the future King George II. Not surprisingly in the circumstances, he made it his business to cultivate the Prince's mistress. The hostility that this friendship aroused in the Prince's wife, later Queen Caroline, herself a confidante of Sir Robert Walpole, has been seen as the reason why, despite his undoubted abilities, Chesterfield never made it to the top of the political ladder.

The times, they may have changed since the 18th Century, but it would be naive to suggest that women have lost their role in making or breaking a man. In recent years there have been many famous falls in fortune involving women, in particular in the political arena – Sara Keays and Cecil Parkinson, Monica Coughlin and Jeffrey Archer, Andreas Papandreou and Dimitri Liani, Sosuke Uno and Mitsuko Nakanishi. And in different circumstances, the woman can still seem to crown a man's career – Maria Calla and Onassis, Greta Garbo and Leopold Stokowski, Mia Farrow and Woody Allen. . .

Since 1975 it has been illegal in Britain to discriminate against women on account of their sex in the context of employment, and it is increasingly the norm to find women in positions of direct power in business and the professions. It is unlikely that appealing to a woman's vanity is a sure fire way to influence her judgment in such contexts. Certainly it would be even more a contentious suggestion today than when the *Letters* were first published, to say so. However, it does not follow from this new state of affairs that the basic principle of Chesterfield's strategy is inapplicable, namely that everyone has a mind to be thought to excel in something – be it beauty, charm, wisdom or judgment – 'touch him but there, and you touch him to the quick'.

You must be sensible that you cannot rise in the world without forming connections and engaging different characters to conspire in your point.

Dear Boy,   *November, 1749*

You must be sensible that you cannot rise in the world without forming connections and engaging different characters to conspire in your point. You must make them your dependants without their knowing it, and dictate to them while you seem to be directed by them. Those necessary connections can never be formed or preserved but by an uninterrupted series of complaisance, attentions, politeness, and some constraint. You must engage their hearts if you would have their support; you must watch the *mollia tempora*, and captivate them by the *agrémens*, and charms of conversation. People will not be called out to your service only when you want them; and, if you expect to receive strength from them, they must receive either pleasure or advantage from you.

I received in this instant a letter from Mr. Harte, of the 2nd, N.S., which I will answer soon; in the mean time I return him my thanks for it, through you. The constant good accounts which he gives me of you will make me suspect him of partiality, and think him *le médecin tant mieux*. Consider, therefore, what weight any future deposition of his against you must necessarily have with me; as, in that case, he will be a very unwilling, he must consequently be a very important witness. Adieu!

Dear Boy,   *March, 1748*
    Intrinsic merit alone will not do; it will gain you the general esteem of all; but not the particular affection, that is, the heart of any. To engage the affection of any particular person, you must, over and above your general merit, have some particular merit to that person, by services done or offered; by expressions of regard and esteem; by complaisance, attentions, etc., for him: and the graceful manner of doing all these things opens the way to the heart, and facilitates, or rather insures, their effects. Adieu.

Dear Boy,   *May, 1749*
    A thousand nameless little things, which nobody can describe, but which everybody feels, conspire to form that *whole* of pleasing; as the several pieces of a mosaic work, though separately of little beauty or value, when properly joined, form those beautiful figures which please everybody. A look, a gesture, an attitude, a tone of voice, all bear their parts in the great work of pleasing. The art of pleasing is more particularly necessary in your intended profession than perhaps in any other; it is in truth the first half of your business; for, if you do not please the Court you are sent to, you will be of very little

'You must be sensible that you cannot rise in the world without forming connections and engaging different characters to conspire to your point.'

use to the Court you are sent from. Please the eyes and the ears, they will introduce you to the heart; and nine times in ten the heart governs the understanding.

Make your court particularly, and show distinguished attentions, to such men and women as are best at Court, highest in the fashion, and in the opinion of the public; speak advantageously of them behind their backs, in companies who you have reason to believe will tell them again. Express your admiration of the many great men that the House of Savoy has produced; observe, that nature, instead of being exhausted by those efforts, seems to have redoubled them in the persons of the present King and the Duke of Savoy: wonder at this rate where it will end, and conclude that it must end in the government of all Europe. Say this, likewise, where it will probably be repeated; but say it unaffectedly, and, the last especially, with a kind of *enjouement*. These little arts are very allowable, and must be made use of in the course of the world; they are pleasing to one party, useful to the other, and injurious to nobody. Adieu

Dear Boy,   *October, 1747*
If you would particularly gain the affection and friendship of particular people, whether men or women, endeavour to find out their predominant excellency, if they have one, and their prevailing weakness, which everybody has; and do justice to the one, and something more than justice to the other. Men have various objects in which they may excel, or at least would be thought to excel; and though they love to hear justice done to them, where they know that they excel, yet they are most and best flattered upon those points where they wish to

Every man talks most of what he has most a mind to be thought to excel in. Touch him but there, and you touch him to the quick.

excel, and yet are doubtful whether they do or not. As for example: Cardinal Richelieu, who was undoubtedly the ablest statesman of his time, or perhaps of any other, had the idle vanity of being thought the best poet too: he envied the great Corneille his reputation, and ordered a criticism to be written upon the *Cid*. Those, therefore, who flattered skilfully, said little to him of his abilities in state affairs, or at least but *en passant*, and as it might naturally occur. But the incense which they gave him— the smoke of which they knew would turn his head in their favour—was as a *bel esprit* and a poet. Why?— Because he was sure of one excellency, and distrustful as to the other.

You will easily discover every man's prevailing vanity by observing his favourite topic of conversation; for every man talks most of what he has most a mind to be thought to excel in. Touch him but there, and you touch him to the quick. The late Sir Robert Walpole (who was certainly an able man) was little open to flattery upon that head, for he was in no doubt himself about it; but his prevailing weakness was, to be thought to have a polite and happy turn to gallantry—of which he had undoubtedly less than any man living. It was his favourite and frequent subject of conversation, which proved to those who had any penetration that it was his prevailing weakness, and they applied to it with success.

Women have, in general, but one object, which is their beauty; upon which, scarce any flattery is too gross for them to follow. Nature has hardly formed a woman ugly enough to be insensible to flattery upon her person; if her face is so shocking that she must, in some degree, be conscious of it, her figure and air, she trusts, make ample amends for it. If her figure is deformed, her face, she thinks, counterbalances it. If they are both bad, she comforts herself that she has graces; a certain manner; a *je ne sçais quoi* still more engaging than beauty. This truth is evident, from the studied and elaborate dress of the ugliest woman in the world. An undoubted, uncontested, conscious beauty is, of all women, the least sensible of flattery upon that head; she knows it is her due, and is therefore obliged to nobody for giving it her. She must be flattered upon her understanding, which, though she may possibly not doubt herself, yet she suspects that men may distrust.

Do not mistake me, and think that I mean to recommend to you abject and criminal flattery: no; flatter nobody's vices or crimes: on the contrary, abhor and discourage them. But there is no living in the world without a complaisant indulgence for people's weaknesses, and innocent, though ridiculous vanities. If a man has a mind to be thought wiser, and a woman handsomer, than they really are, their error is a comfortable one to themselves, and an innocent one with regard to other people; and I would rather make them my friends by indulging them in it, than my enemies by endeavouring (and that to no purpose) to undeceive them.

If a man has a mind to be thought wiser, and a woman handsomer, than they really are . . . I would rather make them my friends by indulging them in it, than my enemies by endeavouring (and that to no purpose) to undeceive them.

Dear Boy,   *September, 1748*

Berlin will be entirely a new scene to you, and I look upon it in a manner as your first step into the great world: take care that step be not a false one, and that you do not stumble at the threshold. You will there be in more company than you have yet been; manners and attentions will therefore be more necessary. Pleasing in company is the only way of being pleased in it yourself. Sense and knowledge are the first and necessary foundations for pleasing in company; but they will by no means do alone, and they will never be perfectly welcome if they are not accompanied with manners and attentions. You will best acquire these by frequenting the companies of people of fashion; but then you must resolve to acquire them in those companies by proper care and observation; for I have known people who, though they have frequented good company all their lifetime, have done it in so inattentive and unobserving a manner as to be never the better for it, and to remain as disagreeable, as awkward, and as vulgar, as if they had never seen any person of fashion. When you go into good company (by good company is meant the people of the first fashion of the place) observe carefully their turn, their manners, their address, and conform your own to them.

As women are a considerable, or at least a pretty numerous part, of company; and as their suffrages go a great way towards establishing a man's character in the fashionable part of the world (which is of great importance to the fortune and figure he proposes to make in it), it is necessary to please them. I will therefore, upon this subject, let you into certain *arcana*, that will be very useful for you to know, but which you must, with the utmost care, conceal, and never seem to know. Women, then, are only children of a larger growth; they have an entertaining tattle and sometimes wit; but for solid, reasoning good-sense, I never in my life knew one that had it, or who reasoned or acted consequentially for four-and-twenty hours together. Some little passion or humour always breaks in upon their best resolutions. Their beauty neglected or controverted, their age increased, or their supposed understandings depreciated, instantly kindles their little passions, and overturns any system of consequential conduct, that in their most reasonable moments they might have been capable of forming. A man of sense only trifles with them, plays with them, humours and flatters them, as he does with a sprightly, forward child;

but he neither consults them about, nor trusts them with, serious matters; though he often makes them believe that he does both; which is the thing in the world that they are proud of; for they love mightily to be dabbling in business (which by the way, they always spoil); and being justly distrustful, that men in general look upon them in a trifling light, they almost adore that man, who talks more seriously to them, and who seems to consult and trust them; I say, who seems, for weak men really do, but wise ones only seem to do it. No flattery is either too high or too low for them. They will greedily swallow the highest, and gratefully accept of the lowest; and you may safely flatter any woman, from her understanding down to the exquisite taste of her fan. Women who are either indisputably beautiful, or indisputably ugly, are best flattered upon the score of their understandings; but those who are in a state of mediocrity, are best flattered upon their beauty, or at least their graces; for every woman who is not absolutely ugly, thinks herself handsome; but, not hearing often that she is so, is the more grateful and the more obliged to the few who tell her so; whereas a decided and conscious beauty looks upon every tribute paid to her beauty, only as her due; but wants to shine, and to be considered on the side of her understanding; and a woman who is ugly enough to know that she is so, knows that she has nothing left for it but her understanding, which is consequently (and probably in more senses than one) her weak side.

But these are secrets which you must keep inviolably, if you would not, like Orpheus, be torn to pieces by the whole sex; on the contrary, a man who thinks of living in the great world, must be gallant, polite, and attentive to please the women. They have, from the weakness of men, more or less influence in all Courts; they absolutely stamp every man's character in the *beau monde*, and make it either current, or cry it down, and stop it in payments. It is, therefore, absolutely necessary to manage, please, and flatter them; and never to discover the least marks of contempt, which is what they never forgive; but in this they are not singular, for it is the same with men; who will much sooner forgive an injustice than an insult. Every man is not ambitious, or covetous, or passionate; but every man has pride enough in his composition to feel and resent the least slight and contempt. Remember, therefore, most carefully to conceal your contempt, however just, wherever you would not make an implacable enemy. Men are much more unwilling to have their weaknesses and their imperfections known, than their crimes; and, if you hint to a man that you think him silly, ignorant, or even ill-bred or awkward, he will hate you more, and longer, than if you tell him plainly that you think him a rogue. Never yield to that temptation, which to most young men is very strong, of exposing other people's weaknesses and infirmities, for the sake either of diverting the company, or of showing your own superiority. You may get the laugh on your side by it, for the present; but you will make enemies by it for ever; and even those who laugh with you then will, upon reflection, fear, and consequently hate you; besides that, it is ill-natured, and a good heart desires rather to conceal than expose other people's weaknesses or misfortunes.

BUSINESS STRATEGY

I n these letters Chesterfield outlines a bedrock strategy, without which no business can proceed. Its watchwords are 'single focus', 'order', and 'efficiency'. If attentiveness is directed towards other people in the development of style, attention is directed towards one's work. Attention is not to be confused with narrow pre-occupation; it is a single-minded focus on the business in hand.

To enable focus, method is required to enslave the demon, Time; as is an understanding of the difference between 'haste' and 'hurry'. The 'cool steadiness' with which 'a man of sense' proceeds is in contrast to the workaholic trapped in a descending spiral of ineffectiveness. There is a modern parallel in the successful Grand Prix driver who develops an ability to see everything as it were in slow motion, in order to make the decisions necessary to win. For the player in the modern 'rat race' of business, the secret lies in developing a method to cope with the little things, lest they become the focus of undue attention or cloud an all-important sense of priorities.

Cool, undemonstrative, back-room efficiency is also the basis of Chesterfield's advice about the writing of business letters. Just as time should be put to effective and economic use, so should language. Circumlocution, poor syntax, and ambiguity, all encourage misinterpretation. Yet business letters are often the final source to be consulted in a dispute.

As in all areas of Chesterfield's plan, the most incidental, most easily overlooked details, are the ones which make the difference and provide the telling edge.

Dear Boy, *April, 1747*

If you feel half the pleasure from the consciousness of doing well, that I do from the informations I have lately received in your favour from Mr. Harte, I shall have little occasion to exhort or admonish you any more, to do what your own satisfaction and self-love will sufficiently prompt you to. Mr. Harte tells me that you attend, that you apply to your studies; and that, beginning to understand, you begin to taste them. This pleasure will increase, and keep pace with your attention; so that the balance will be greatly to your advantage.

You may remember, that I have always earnestly recommended to you to do what you are about, be that what it will; and to do nothing else at the same time. Do not imagine that I mean, by this, that you should attend to, and plod at, your book all day long; far from it: I mean that you should have your pleasures too; and that you should attend to them, for the time, as much as to your studies; and, if you do not attend equally to both, you will neither have improvement nor satisfaction from either. A man is fit for neither business nor pleasure, who either cannot, or does not, command and direct his attention to the present object, and, in some degree, banish, for that time, all other objects from his thoughts. If at a ball, a supper, or a party of pleasure, a man were to be solving, in his own mind, a problem in Euclid, he would be a very bad companion, and make a very poor figure in that company; or if, in studying a problem in his closet, he were to think of a minuet, I am apt to believe that he would make a very poor mathematician. There is time enough for every thing in the course of the day, if you do but one thing at once; but there is not time enough in the year, if you will do two things at a time.

The Pensionary de Witt, who was torn to pieces in the year 1672, did the whole business of the Republic, and yet had time left to go to assemblies in the evening, and sup in company. Being asked how he could possibly find time to go through so much business, and yet amuse himself in the evenings as he did? he answered, "There was nothing so easy; for that it was only doing one thing at a time, and never putting off anything till to-morrow that could be done to-day." This steady and undissipated attention to one object, is a sure mark of a superior genius; as hurry, bustle, and agitation, are the never-failing symptoms of a weak and frivolous mind.

Whoever is in a hurry, shows that the thing he is about is too big for him. Haste and hurry are very different things.

Dear Boy,   *January, 1751*

A man of sense may be in haste, but can never be in a hurry, because he knows, that whatever he does in a hurry he must necessarily do very ill. He may be in haste to despatch an affair, but he will take care not to let that haste hinder his doing it well. Little minds are in a

'Whoever is in a hurry, shows that the thing he is about is too big for him. Haste and hurry are very different things.'

hurry, when the object proves (as it commonly does) too big for them; they run, they hare, they puzzle, confound, and perplex themselves; they want to do everything at once, and never do it at all. But a man of sense takes the time necessary for doing the thing he is about well: and his haste to despatch a business, only appears by the continuity of his application to it: he pursues it with a cool steadiness, and finishes it before he begins any other. I own your time is much taken up, and you have a great many different things to do; but remember, that you had much better do half of them well, and leave the other half undone, than do them all indifferently. Moreover, the few seconds that are saved in the course of the day, by writing ill instead of well, do not amount to an object of time, by any means equivalent to the disgrace or ridicule of writing such a scrawl. Consider, that if your very bad writing could furnish me with matter of ridicule, what will it not do to others, who do not view you in the same light that I do.

Dear Boy,   *February, 1750*

Very few people are good economists of their fortune, and still fewer of their time; and yet of the two the latter is the most precious. I heartily wish you to be a good economist of both; and you are now of an age to begin to think seriously of these two important articles. Young people are apt to think they have so much time before them, that they may squander what they please of it, and yet have enough left; as very great fortunes have frequently seduced people to a ruinous profusion: fatal mistakes! always repented of, but always too late! Old Mr. Lowndes, the famous Secretary of the Treasury in the reigns of King William, Queen Anne, and King George the First, used to say, *take care of the pence, and the pounds will take care of themselves.* To this maxim, which he not only preached but practised, his two grandsons at this time owe the very considerable fortunes that he left them.

The value of moments, when cast up, is immense, if well employed; if thrown away, their loss is irrecoverable.

This holds equally true as to time; and I most earnestly recommend to you the care of those minutes and quarters of hours, in the course of the day, which people think too short to deserve their attention; and yet, if summed up at the end of the year, would amount to a very considerable portion of time. For example: you are to be at such a place at twelve, by appointment; you go out at eleven to make two or three visits first; those persons are not at home; instead of sauntering away that intermediate time at a coffee-house, and possibly alone, return home, write a letter, beforehand, for the ensuing post, or take up a book. By these means (to use a city metaphor) you will make fifty *per cent.* of that time of which others do not make above three or four, or probably nothing at all.

Many people lose a great deal of their time by laziness; they loll and yawn in a great chair, tell themselves that they have not time to begin anything then, and that it will do as well another time. This is a most unfortunate disposition, and the greatest obstruction to both knowledge and business. At your age, you have no right nor claim to laziness; I have, if I please, being *emeritus*. You are but just listed in the world, and must be active, diligent, indefatigable. If ever you propose commanding with dignity, you must serve up to it with diligence. Never put off till to-morrow what you can do to-day.

---

*D*espatch is the soul of business; and nothing contributes more to Despatch than Method.

Despatch is the soul of business; and nothing contributes more to Despatch, than Method. Lay down a method for everything, and stick to it inviolably, as far as unexpected incidents may allow. Fix one certain hour and day in the week for your accounts, and keep them together in their proper order; by which means they will require very little time, and you can never be much cheated. Whatever letters and papers you keep, docket and tie them up in their respective classes, so that you may instantly have recourse to any one. Lay down a method also for your reading, for which you allot a certain share of your mornings; let it be in a consistent and consecutive course, and not in that desultory and immethodical manner, in which many people read scraps of different authors, upon different subjects.

Keep a useful and short common-place book of what you read, to help your memory only, and not for pedantic quotations. Never read History without having maps, and a chronological book, or tables, lying by you, and constantly recurred to; without which, History is only a confused heap of facts. One method more I recommend to you by which I have found great benefit, even in the most dissipated part of my life; that is, to rise early, and at the same hour every morning, how late soever you may have sat up the night before. This secures you an hour or two, at least, of reading or reflection, before the common interruptions of the morning begin; and it will save your constitution, by forcing you to go to bed early, at least one night in three.

You will say, it may be, as many young people would, that all this order and method is very troublesome, only fit for dull people, and a disagreeable restraint upon the noble spirit and fire of youth. I deny it; and assert, on the contrary, that it will procure you, both more time and more taste for your pleasures; and, so far from being troublesome to you, that, after you have pursued it a month, it would be troublesome to you to lay it aside. Adieu!

Dear Boy, *January, 1749*

A fool squanders away, without credit or advantage to himself, more than a man of sense spends with both. The latter employs his money as he does his time, and never spends a shilling of the one, nor a minute of the other, but in something that is either useful or rationally pleasing to himself or others; the former buys whatever

The man of sense employs his money as he does his time, and never spends a shilling of the one or a minute of the other, but in something that is either useful or rationally pleasing to himself or others.

he does not want, and does not pay for what he does want. He cannot withstand the charms of a toy-shop; snuff-boxes, watches, heads of canes, etc., are his destruction. His servants and tradesmen conspire with his own indolence to cheat him; and in a very little time he is astonished, in the midst of all the ridiculous superfluities, to find himself in want of all the real comforts and necessaries of life. Without care and method, the largest fortune will not—and with them, almost the smallest will—supply all necessary expenses. As far as you can possibly, pay ready money for everything you buy, and avoid bills. Pay that money, too, yourself, and not through the hands of any servant, who always either stipulates poundage, or requires a present for his good word, as they call it. Where you must have bills (as for meat and drink, clothes, etc.), pay them regularly every month, and with your own hand. Never, from a mistaken economy, buy a thing you do not want because it is cheap, or, from a silly pride, because it is dear. Keep an account in a book of all that you receive, and of all that you pay; for no man, who knows what he receives and what he pays, ever runs out. I do not mean that you should keep an account of the shillings and half-crowns which you may spend in chair-hire, operas, etc.; they are unworthy of the time, and of the ink, that they would consume. Leave such *minuties* to dull, penny-wise fellows; but remember, in economy, as well as in every other part of life, to have the proper attention to proper objects, and the proper contempt for little ones.

The trifling and frivolous mind is always busied, but to little purpose; it takes little objects for great ones, and throws away upon trifles that time and attention, which only important things deserve.

A strong mind sees things in their true proportions; a weak one views them through a magnifying medium, which, like the microscope, makes an elephant of a flea, magnifies all little objects, but cannot receive great ones. I have known many a man pass for a miser, by saving a penny and wrangling for twopence, who was undoing himself at the same time by living above his income, and not attending to essential articles, which were above his *portée*. The sure characteristic of a sound and strong mind is, to find in everything those certain bounds, *quos ultra citraque nequit consistere rectum.* These boundaries are marked out by a very fine line, which only good sense and attention can discover: it is much too fine for vulgar eyes. In manners, this line is good-breeding; beyond it, is troublesome ceremony, short of it, is unbecoming negligence and inattention. In morals, it divides ostentatious puritanism from criminal relaxation. In religion, superstition from impiety; and, in short, every virtue from its kindred vice or weakness. I think you have sense enough to discover the line: keep it always in your eye, and learn to walk upon it; rest upon Mr. Harte, and he will poise you till you are able to go alone. By the way, there are fewer people who walk well upon that line than upon the slack rope, and therefore a good performer shines so much the more.

Dear Boy,   *December, 1751*

You are now entered upon a scene of business, where I hope you will one day make a figure. Use does a great deal, but care and attention must be joined to it. The first thing necessary in writing letters of business is extreme clearness and perspicuity; every paragraph should be so clear and unambiguous, that the dullest fellow in the world may not be able to mistake it, nor obliged to read it twice in order to understand it. This necessary clearness implies a correctness, without excluding elegancy of style. Tropes, figures, antitheses, epigrams, etc., would be as misplaced and as impertinent in letters of business, as they are sometimes (if judiciously used) proper and pleasing in familiar letters, upon common and trite subjects. In business, an elegant simplicity, the result of care, not of labour is required.

Business must be well, not affectedly, dressed, but by no means negligently. Let your first attention be to clearness, and read every paragraph after you have written it, in the critical view of discovering whether it is possible that any one man can mistake the true sense of it; and correct it accordingly.

Our pronouns and relatives often create obscurity or ambiguity; be therefore exceedingly attentive to them, and take care to mark out with precision their particular relations. For example, Mr. Johnson acquainted me that he had seen Mr. Smith, who had promised him to speak to Mr. Clarke, to return him (Mr. Johnson) those papers which he (Mr. Smith) had left some time ago with him (Mr. Clarke); it is better to repeat a name, though unnecessarily, ten times, than to have the person mistaken once. *Who*, you know, is singly relative to persons, and cannot be applied to things; *which* and *that* are chiefly relative to things, but not absolutely exclusive of persons; for one may say, the man *that* robbed or killed such-a-one; but it is much better to say, the man *who* robbed or killed. One never says, the man or the woman *which*. *Which* and *that*, though chiefly relative to things, cannot be always used indifferently as to things; and the εὐφωνία must sometimes determine their place. For instance: The letter *which* I received from you, *which* you referred to in your last, *which* came by Lord Albemarle's messenger, and *which* I showed to such-a-person; I would change it thus: The letter *that* I received from you, *which* you referred to in your last, *that* came by Lord Albemarle's messenger, and *which* I showed to such-a-one.

Business does not exclude (as possibly you wish it

did) the usual terms of politeness and good-breeding, but, on the contrary, strictly requires them; such as, *I have the honour to acquaint your Lordship; Permit me to assure you; If I may be allowed to give my opinion,* etc. For the Minister abroad, who writes to the Minister at home, writes to his superior; possibly to his patron, or at least to one who he desires should be so.

Letters of business will not only admit of, but be the better for *certain graces*: but then, they must be scattered with a sparing and a skilful hand; they must fit their places exactly. They must decently adorn without encumbering, and modestly shine without glaring. But as this is the utmost degree of perfection in letters of business, I would not advise you to attempt those embellishments till you have first laid your foundation well.

Cardinal d'Ossat's letters are the true letters of business; those of Monsieur D'Avaux are excellent; Sir William Temple's are very pleasing, but I fear too affected. Carefully avoid all Greek or Latin quotations; and bring no precedents from the *virtuous Spartans, the polite Athenians, and the brave Romans.* Leave all that to futile pedants. No flourishes, no declamation. But (I repeat it again) there is an elegant simplicity and dignity of style absolutely necessary for good letters of business; attend to that carefully. Let your periods be harmonious, without seeming to be laboured; and let them not be too long, for that always occasions a degree of obscurity. I should not mention correct orthography, but that you very often fail in that particular, which will bring ridicule upon you; for no man is allowed to spell ill. I wish too that your handwriting were much better, and I cannot conceive why it is not, since every man may certainly write whatever hand he pleases. Neatness in folding up, sealing, and directing your packets, is by no means to be neglected; though I dare say you think it is. But there is something in the exterior, even of a packet, that may please or displease; and consequently be worth some attention.

You say that your time is very well employed, and so it is, though as yet only in the outlines, and first *routine* of business. They are previously necessary to be known; they smooth the way for parts and dexterity. Business requires no conjuration nor supernatural talents, as people unacquainted with it are apt to think. Method, diligence, and discretion, will carry a man of good strong common sense much higher than the finest parts, without them, can do. *Par negotiis, neque supra*, is the true character of a man of business; but then it implies ready attention, and no *absences*; and a flexibility and versatility of attention from one object to another, without being engrossed by any one.

Be upon your guard against the pedantry and affectation of business, which young people are apt to fall into, from the pride of being concerned in it young. They look thoughtful, complain of the weight of business, throw out mysterious hints, and seem big with secrets which they do not know. Do you on the contrary never talk of business but to those with whom you are to transact it; and learn to seem *vacuus* and idle when you have the most business. Of all things, the *volto sciolto* and the *pensieri stretti* are necessary. Adieu!

THE ART OF NEGOTIATION

8

'In business, how prevalent are the Graces, how detrimental is the want of them!... The utility of them in negotiations is inconceivable.'

N egotiation was essential to Philip's planned career as diplomat and politician, and indeed to any business at all. Chesterfield himself achieved considerable success through negotiation. In his first three years at the Hague he prevented war with Prussia, organised the preliminaries to the marriage of the Prince of Orange and the Princess Royal, and carried on secret talks with the Austrian envoy, Count Sinzendorf, which led to the Second Treaty of Vienna. His period of time as Lord Lieutenant of Ireland was perhaps the best in the country's history.

Chesterfield uses two phrases – *fortiter in re* and *suaviter in modo* – to describe the essential ingredients of successful negotiation, whether in business or politics. Roughly they stand for 'resolution' and 'a pleasant manner', respectively. Overall, his strategy is not dissimilar to that of 'the iron fist and the velvet glove'. Without unassailable resolution, the value of a deal – your profit and loss account – may be compromised; but without displaying consideration for the profit and loss account of your opponent's sensitivities, it is more or less difficult to secure his agreement, depending on the strength of your position. *Suaviter in modo* is clearly essential when arguing from a weak position, but there is an implication that even when arguing from a position of strength it remains important, especially if you may wish to do business with him in the future.

Again, a measure of character analysis is in order – 'The knowledge of mankind is very useful. . . You will have to do with all sorts of characters; you should, therefore, know them thoroughly in order to manage them ably. . . Seek first, then, for the predominant passion of the character which you mean to engage and influence, and address yourself to it. . . There are many avenues to every man. . .'

Equally, since negotiation is a two-way process, attend to your own performance so as not to leave yourself open to manipulation. Stand outside yourself, analyse your own performance as an opponent might, listen not to what you say but how you think your opponent would 'hear' what you say. Pomposity and egotism lay you open to manipulation, a quick temper is the surest road to failure.

Fortiter in re and *suaviter in modo* reach to the core of Chesterfield's system, recalling the solid foundation of knowledge overlaid with the evanescent charms of style. The latter is the mode in which the former is put to work.

A common feature throughout Chesterfield's system – and a characteristic of *suaviter in modo* – is 'ease'. As elsewhere, in negotiation Chesterfield suggests ways of defusing tension, none of which are to be confused with obsequiousness: 'I do not mean to recommend to you *le fade doucereux*, the insipid softness of a gentle fool; no, assert your own opinion, oppose other people's when wrong; but let your manner, your air, your terms, and your tone of voice, be soft and gentle, and that easily and naturally, not affectedly. Use palliatives when you contradict; such as, *I may be mistaken; I am not sure, but I believe; I should rather think*, etc. Finish any argument or dispute with some little good-humoured pleasantry, to show that you are neither hurt yourself, nor meant to hurt your antagonist; for an argument kept up a good while often occasions a temporary alienation on each side.'

Dear Boy,   *March, 1751*

I mentioned to you, some time ago, a sentence, which I would most earnestly wish you always to retain in your thoughts and observe in your conduct. It is *suaviter in modo, fortiter in re*. I do not know any one rule so unexceptionally useful and necessary in every part of life. I shall therefore take it for my text to-day; and as old men love preaching, and I have some right to preach to you, I here present you with my sermon upon these words. To proceed then regularly and *pulpitically*; I will first show you, my beloved, the necessary connexion of the two members of my text, *suaviter in modo, fortiter in re*. In the next place, I shall set forth the advantages and utility resulting from a strict observance of the precept contained in my text; and conclude with an application of the whole. The *suaviter in modo* alone would degenerate and sink into a mean, timid complaisance, and passiveness, if not supported and dignified by the *fortiter in re*; which would also run into impetuosity and brutality if not tempered and softened by the *suaviter in modo*; however, they are seldom united. The warm choleric man with strong animal spirits despises the *suaviter in modo*, and thinks to carry all before him by the *fortiter in re*. He may, possibly, by great accidents, now and then succeed, when he has only weak and timid people to deal with; but his general fate will be to shock, offend, be hated, and fail. On the other hand, the cunning, crafty man, thinks to gain all ends by the *suaviter in modo* only: *he becomes all things to all men*; he seems to have no opinion of his own, and servilely adopts the present opinion of the present person; he insinuates himself only into the esteem of fools, but is soon detected, and surely despised by everybody else. The wise man (who differs as much from the cunning as from the choleric man) alone joins the *suaviter in modo* with the *fortiter in re.*

Now to the advantages arising from the strict observance of this precept. If you are in authority, and have a right to command, your commands delivered *suaviter in modo* will be willingly, cheerfully, and consequently well obeyed; whereas, if given only *fortiter*, that is brutally, they will rather, as Tacitus says, be interpreted than executed. For my own part, if I bid my footman bring me a glass of wine in a rough, insulting manner, I should expect that in obeying me he would contrive to spill some of it upon me; and I am sure I should deserve it. A cool steady resolution should show, that where you have a right to command you will be obeyed; but, at the same time, a gentleness in the manner of enforcing that obedience should make it a cheerful one, and soften, as much as possible, the mortifying consciousness of inferiority. If you are to ask a favour, or even to solicit your due, you must do it *suaviter in modo,* or you will give those who have a mind to refuse you either, a pretence to do it by resenting the manner; but, on the other hand, you must, by a steady perseverance and decent tenaciousness, show the *fortiter in re.*

The right motives are seldom the true ones of men's actions, especially of kings, ministers, and people in high stations; who often give to importunity, and fear what they would refuse to justice or to merit. By the *suaviter in modo* engage their hearts, if you can; at least, prevent the pretence of offence; but take care to show enough of the *fortiter in re* to extort from their love of ease, or their fear, what you might in vain hope for from their justice or good-nature. People in high life are hardened to the wants and distresses of mankind as surgeons are to their bodily pains; they see and hear of them all day long, and even of so many simulated ones, that they do not know which are real and which not. Other sentiments are therefore to be applied to than those of mere justice and humanity; their favour must be captivated by the *suaviter in modo*; their love of ease disturbed by unwearied importunity, or their fears wrought upon by a decent intimation of impacable, cool resentment; this is the true *fortiter in re*. This precept is the only way I know in the world of being loved without being despised, and feared without being hated. It constitutes the dignity of character, which every wise man must endeavour to establish.

Now to apply what has been said, and so conclude.

Let no weak desire of pleasing on your part, no wheedling, coaxing, nor flattery, on other people's, make you recede one jot from any point that reason and prudence bid you pursue.

If you find that you have a hastiness in your temper, which unguardedly breaks out into indiscreet sallies or rough expressions, to either your superiors, your equals, or your inferiors, watch it narrowly, check it carefully, and call the *suaviter in modo* to your assistance; at the first impulse of passion be silent till you can be soft. Labour even to get the command of your countenance so well, that those emotions may not be read in it; a most unspeakable advantage in business. On the other hand, let no complaisance, no gentleness of temper, no weak desire of pleasing on your part, no wheedling, coaxing, nor flattery, on other people's, make you recede one jot from any point that reason and prudence have bid you pursue; but return to the charge, persist, persevere, and you will find most things attainable that are possible. Adieu!

Dear Boy,   *September, 1752*
    When I went to the Hague, in 1744, it was to engage the Dutch to come roundly into the war, and to stipulate their quotas of troops, etc.; your acquaintance, the Abbé de la Ville, was there on the part of France, to endeavour to hinder them from coming into the war at all. I was informed, and very sorry to hear it, that he had abilities, temper, and industry. We could not visit, our two masters being at war; but the first time I met him at a third place, I got somebody to present me to him; and I told him, that though we were to be national enemies, I flattered myself we might be, however, personal friends; with a good deal more of the same kind, which he returned in full as polite a manner. Two days afterwards I went, early in the morning, to solicit the deputies of Amsterdam, where I found l'Abbé de la Ville, who had been beforehand with me; upon which I addressed

myself to the Deputies, and said, smilingly, *Je suis bien fâché, Messieurs, de trouver mon ennemi avec vous; je le connois déjà assez pour le craindre; la partie n'est pas égale, mais je me fie à vos propres intérêts contre les talens de mon ennemi; et au moins si je n'ai pas eu le premier mot j'aurai le dernier aujourd'hui.* They smiled; the Abbé was pleased with the compliment, and the manner of it, stayed about a quarter of an hour, and then left me to my Deputies, with whom I continued upon the same tone, though in a very serious manner, and told them that I was only come to state their own true interests to them, plainly and simply, without any of those arts, which it was very necessary for my friend to make use of to deceive them. I carried my point, and continued my *procédé* with the Abbé; and by this easy and polite commerce with him, at third places, I often found means to fish out from him whereabouts he was.

Remember, there are but two *procédés* in the world for a gentleman and a man of parts; either extreme politeness or knocking down. If a man, notoriously and designedly insults and affronts you, knock him down; but if he only injures you, your best revenge is to be extremely civil to him in your outward behaviour, though at the same time you counterwork him, and return him the compliment, perhaps with interest. This is not perfidy nor dissimulation; it would be so, if you were at the same time, to make professions of esteem and friendship to this man, which I by no means recommend, but, on the contrary, abhor. All acts of civility are, by common consent, understood to be no more than a conformity to custom, for the quiet and conveniency of society, the *agrémens* of which are not to be disturbed by private dislikes and jealousies. Only women and little minds pout and spar for the entertainment of the company, that always laughs at, and never pities them. For my own part, though I would by no means give up any point to a competitor, yet I would pique myself upon showing him rather more civility than to another man. In the first place, this *procédé* infallibly makes all *les rieurs* of your side, which is a considerable party; and in the next place, it certainly pleases the object of the competition, be it either man or woman; who never fail to say, upon such occasion, that *they must own you have behaved yourself very handsomely in the whole affair.*

Do not trust to appearances and outside yourself, but pay other people with them; because you may be sure that 9 out of 10 of mankind do, and ever will, trust to them.

Dear Boy,   *May, 1751*

Mankind, as I have often told you, is more governed by appearances, than by realities . . . One had better be really rough and hard, with the appearance of gentleness and softness, than just the reverse. Few people have penetration enough to discover, attention enough to observe, or even concern enough to examine, beyond the exterior; they take their notions from the surface, and go no deeper; they commend, as the gentlest and best-natured man in the world, that man who has the most engaging exterior manner, though possibly they have been but once in their company. An air, a tone of voice, a composure of countenance to mildness and softness, which are all easily acquired, do the business . . . Do not therefore trust to appearances and outside yourself, but pay other people with them; because you may be sure that nine in ten of mankind do, and ever will, trust to them.

This is by no means a criminal or blameable simulation, if not used with an ill intention.

We must not suppose, that because a man is a rational animal, he will, therefore, always act rationally.

Dear Boy,   *December, 1749*

The knowledge of mankind is a very useful knowledge for everybody—a most necessary one for you, who are destined to an active public life. You will have to do with all sorts of characters; you should, therefore, know them thoroughly in order to manage them ably. This knowledge is not to be gotten systematically, you must acquire it yourself by your own observation and sagacity: I will give you such hints as I think may be useful landmarks in your intended progress. I have often told you (and it is most true) that, with regard to mankind, we must not draw general conclusions from certain particular principles, though in the main, true ones. We must not suppose, that because a man is a rational animal, he will, therefore, always act rationally; or, because he has such or such a predominant passion, that he will act invariably and consequentially in the pursuit of it. No; we are complicated machines; and though we have one main-spring that gives motion to the whole, we have an infinity of little wheels, which in their turns, retard, precipitate, and sometimes stop that motion. Let us exemplify: I will suppose ambition to be (as it commonly is) the predominant passion of a minister of state, and I will suppose that minister to be an able one; will he, therefore, invariably pursue the object of that predominant passion? May I be sure that he will do so and so, because he ought? Nothing less. Sickness, or low spirits, may damp this predominant passion; humour and peevishness may triumph over it; inferior passions may at times surprise it and prevail. Is this

Seek first, then, for the predominant passion of the character which you mean to engage and influence, and address yourself to it.

ambitious statesman amorous? indiscreet and un-guarded confidences, made in tender moments, to his wife or his mistress, may defeat all his schemes. Is he avaricious? some great lucrative object suddenly presenting itself may unravel all the work of his ambition. Is he passionate? contradiction and provocation (sometimes, it may be, too, artfully intended) may exort rash and inconsiderate expressions, or actions, destructive of his main object. Is he vain and open to flattery? an artful flattering favourite may mislead him; and even laziness may, at certain moments, make him neglect or omit the necessary steps to that height which he wants to arrive at. Seek first, then, for the predominant passion of the character which you mean to engage and influence, and address yourself to it; but without defying or despising the inferior passions; get them in your interest too, for now and then they will have their turns. In many cases you may not have it in your power to contribute to the gratification of the prevailing passion; then take the next best to your aid. There are many avenues to every man, and when you cannot get at him through the great one, try the serpentine ones, and you will arrive at last. Adieu!

You must look into people, as well as at them.

Dear Boy   *October, 1746*
   You must look into people, as well as at them. Almost all people are born with all the passions, to a certain degree; but almost every man has a prevailing one, to which the others are subordinate. Search every one for that ruling passion; pry into the recesses of his heart,

and observe the different workings of the same passion in different people. And, when you have found out the prevailing passion of any man, remember never to trust him where that passion is concerned. Work upon him by it, if you please; but be upon your guard yourself against it, whatever professions he may make you. Adieu!

Dear Boy,   *May, 1749*

In any point, which prudence bids you pursue . . . let difficulties only animate your industry, not deter you from the pursuit. If one way has failed, try another; be active, persevere, and you will conquer. Some people are to be reasoned, some flattered, some intimidated, and some teased into a thing; but, in general, all are to be brought into it at last, if skilfully applied to, properly managed, and indefatigably attacked in their several weak places. The time should likewise be judiciously chosen. Every man has his *mollia tempora*, but that is far from being all day long; and you would choose your time very ill, if you applied to a man about one business, when his head was full of another, or when his heart was full of grief, anger, or any other disagreeable sentiment.

Observe, with the utmost attention, all the operations of your own mind . . . and the various motives that determine your will.

In order to judge of the inside of others, study your

own; for men in general are very much alike; and though one has one prevailing passion, and another has another, yet their operations are much the same; and whatever engages or disgusts, pleases or offends you in others, will, *mutatis mutandis*, engage, disgust, please, or offend others in you. Observe, with the utmost attention, all the operations of your own mind, the nature of your own passions, and the various motives that determine your will; and you may, in a great degree, know all mankind. For instance, do you find yourself hurt and mortified, when another makes you feel his superiority, and your own inferiority, in knowledge, parts, rank, or fortune? You will certainly take great care not to make a person whose good-will, good word, interest, esteem, or friendship, you would gain, feel that superiority in you, in case you have it. If disagreeable insinuations, sly sneers, or repeated contradictions tease and irritate you, would you use them where you wished to engage or please? Surely not; and I hope you wish to engage, and please, almost universally. Adieu!

Dear Boy,   *December 1749*

Women are much more like each other than men; they have, in truth, but two passions, vanity and love; these are their universal characteristics. An Agrippina may sacrifice them to ambition, or a Messalina to lust, but such instances are rare; and in general, all they say and all they do tends to the gratification of their vanity or their love. He who flatters them most pleases them best; and they are most in love with him who they think is the most in love with them. No adulation is too strong for them; no assiduity too great; no simulation of passion too gross: as, on the other hand, the least word or action that can possibly be construed into a slight or contempt, is unpardonable, and never forgotten. Men are, in this respect, tender too, and will sooner forgive an injury than an insult. Some men are more captious than others; some are always wrong-headed; but every man living has such a share of vanity as to be hurt by marks of slight and contempt. Every man does not pretend to be a poet, a mathematician, or a statesman, and considered as such; but every man pretends to common sense, and to fill his place in the world with common decency; and consequently does not easily forgive those negligences, inattentions, and slights, which seem to call in question or utterly deny him both these pretensions. Adieu!

Dear Boy,   *May, 1750*

To come now to a point of much less, but yet of very great consequence, at your first setting out. Be extremely upon your guard against vanity, the common failing of inexperienced youth; but particularly against that kind of vanity that dubs a man a coxcomb; a character which, once acquired, is more indelible than that of the priesthood. It is not to be imagined by how many different ways vanity defeats its own purposes. One man decides peremptorily upon every subject, betrays his ignorance upon many, and shows a disgusting presumption upon the rest. Another desires to appear successful among the women; he hints at the encouragement he has received from those of the most distinguished rank and beauty, and intimates a particular connection with some one; if it is true, it is ungenerous; if false, it is infamous; but in either case he destroys the reputation

'Dexterity enough to conceal a truth, without telling a lie; sagacity
enough to read other people's countenances; and serenity enough not

to let them discover anything of yours – these are the rudiments of a politician.'

he wants to get. Be inwardly firm and steady, know your own value, whatever it may be, and act upon that principle; but take great care to let nobody discover that you do know your own value. Whatever real merit you have other people will discover; and people always magnify their own discoveries, as they lessen those of others.

Dear Boy,   *January, 1748*

There are some additional qualifications necessary, in the practical part of business, which may deserve some consideration in your leisure moments—such as, an absolute command of your temper, so as not to be provoked to passion upon any account; patience, to hear frivolous, impertinent, and unreasonable applications; with address enough to refuse, without offending; or, by your manner of granting, to double the obligation;—dexterity enough to conceal a truth, without telling a lie; sagacity enough to read other people's countenances; and serenity enough not to let them discover anything by yours—a seeming frankness, with a real reserve. These are the rudiments of a politician; the world must be your grammar.

Three mails are now due from Holland, so that I have no letters from you to acknowledge. I therefore conclude with recommending myself to your favour and protection when you succeed.   Yours.

THE UTILITY OF MORAL SENSE

CHAPTER

9

Chesterfield's strategy for success has had its critics –
'The unreality and unsatisfactoriness of his system
lay . . . in its pure paganism. His whole philosophy is of the
world, worldly. Of the spiritual, of the transcendental . . . it
has nothing.' (*Coxon*) Chesterfield's strategy *is* of the world –
it is concerned with advancing his son in purely careerist
terms and is an education in the ways of the world, but to
regard Chesterfield as an advocate of immorality, even
atheism, is a mistake. His starting point may have been
worldly, but he arrived at a moral conclusion of sorts.

He acknowledges that his treatment of moral matters is
cursory. But this was to be expected since the letters – not
intended for publication and not published until after
Chesterfield's death – were meant to be a supplement to
Philip's moral and academic education at the hands of his
tutors. To consider Chesterfield's system independently of
the rest of the boy's education can only make it seem more
cynical than was intended. Chesterfield realised the ease with
which superficial accomplishments could become detached
from any real qualities – it was a failing typical of his day –
'Too often the beau and man of fashion lightly concealed
under a thin veneer of polish the heart of a scoundrel.'
(*Turberville*)

However, he was equally aware of the inconvenience of
rigid moral codes, and recommends Philip to avoid becoming
a sententious prig. Nothing is more likely to dry up
conversation than someone flaunting a sense of moral

superiority. For Chesterfield, in all things, utility was the key word. He seeks to justify moral values at the altar of Reason rather than at the altar of Religion. His starting point – 'Is an ethical approach of any practical use?' – may seem suspect, but his conclusion is unassailable: 'For God's sake, be scrupulously jealous of the purity of your moral character.' Moreover, while he reasons that without a spotless moral character Philip will be 'looked upon as a liar, and a trickster, no confidence will be placed in you, nothing will be communicated to you. . .', he specifically rejects the idea that 'all notions of moral good or evil . . . are merely local, and depend entirely upon the customs and fashions of different countries'. The suggestion is, that he shared with religious thinkers a belief in absolute moral values.

Nevertheless, the down-to-earth philosophy of a practical man more often seeks justification in precedent, rather than in judgment of a higher order, as his discussion of the relative merits of 'simulation' and 'dissimulation' – two business tactics – shows. 'Simulation' is falsehood and disallowed, but 'dissimulation', which, in the immortal words of Sir Robert Armstrong (used when seeking to ban Peter Wright's book *Spycatcher*), means 'being economical with the truth', and receives his blessing: 'It may be objected, that I am now recommending dissimulation to you; I both own and justify it . . . I go still farther, and say, that without some dissimulation no business can be carried on at all. It is simulation that is false, mean, and criminal; that is the cunning which Lord Bacon calls crooked or left-handed wisdom. And the same great man says, that dissimulation is only to hide our own cards; whereas simulation is put on in order to look into other people's . . . Dissimulation is a shield, as secrecy is armour, and it is no more possible to preserve secrecy in business, without some degree of dissimulation, than it is to succeed in business without secrecy. . . Those two arts of dissimulation and secrecy are like the alloy mingled with pure ore: a little is necessary, and will not debase the coin below its proper standard; but if more than that little be employed (that is, simulation and cunning), the coin loses its currency and the coiner his credit.'

In the end, Chesterfield's real interest is in how things go on in the world, his criterion for virtue is utility, but there is little doubt as to who should be its beneficiary.

If, in negotiations, you are looked upon as a liar . . . you will be in the situation of a man who has been burnt in the cheek; and who, from that mark, cannot afterwards get an honest livelihood if he would, but must continue a thief.

Dear Boy,   *January, 1750*

If in negotiations, you are looked upon as a liar, and a trickster, no confidence will be placed in you, nothing will be communicated to you, and you will be in the situation of a man who has been burnt in the cheek; and who, from that mark, cannot afterwards get an honest livelihood if he would, but must continue a thief.

Lord Bacon very justly makes a distinction between Simulation and Dissimulation, and allows the latter rather than the former; but still observes, that they are the weaker sort of politicians who have recourse to either. A man who has strength of mind, and strength of parts, wants neither of them. "Certainly," says he, "the ablest men that ever were, have all had an openness and frankness of dealing, and a name of certainty and veracity; but then, they were like horses well-managed, for they could tell, passing well, when to stop, or turn: and at such times, when they thought the case indeed required dissimulation, if then they used it, it came to pass that the former opinion spread abroad, of their good faith and clearness of dealing, made them almost invisible."

It is most certain, that the reputation of chastity is not so necessary for a woman, as that of veracity is for a man; and with reason; for it is possible for a woman to be virtuous, though not strictly chaste; but it is not possible for a man to be virtuous without strict veracity.

For God's sake, be scrupulously jealous of the purity of your moral character; keep it immaculate, unblemished, unsullied.

The slips of the poor women are sometimes mere bodily frailties; but a lie in a man is a vice of the mind, and of the heart. For God's sake, be scrupulously jealous of the purity of your moral character; keep it immaculate, unblemished, unsullied; and it will be unsuspected. Defamation and calumny never attack, where there is no weak place; they magnify, but they do not create. Adieu!

Dear Boy   *May, 1750*

Your apprenticeship is near out, and you are soon to set up for yourself; that approaching moment is a critical one for you, and an anxious one for me. A tradesman who would succeed in his way must begin by establishing a character of integrity and good manners; without the former, nobody will go to his shop at all; without the latter, nobody will go there twice. This rule does not exclude the fair arts of trade. He may sell his goods at the best price he can within certain bounds. He may avail himself of the humour, the whims, and the fantastical tastes of his customers; but what he warrants to be good must be really so, what he seriously asserts must be true, or his first fraudulent profits will soon end in a bankruptcy. It is the same in higher life, and in the great business of the world. A man who does not solidly establish and really deserve a character of truth, probity, good manners, and good morals, at his first setting out in the world, may impose and shine like a meteor for a very short time, but will very soon vanish, and be extinguished with contempt.

People easily pardon, in young men, the common irregularities of the senses; but they do not forgive the least vice of the heart. The heart never grows better by age; I fear rather worse, always harder. A young liar will be an old one, and a young knave will only be a greater knave as he grows older. But should a bad young heart, accompanied with a good head (which, by the way, very seldom is the case), really reform in a more advanced age from a consciousness of its folly, as well as of its guilt, such a conversion would only be thought prudential and political, but never sincere. I hope in God, and I verily believe, that you want no moral virtue. But the possession of all the moral virtues, *in actu primo*, as the logicians call it, is not sufficient; you must have *in actu secundo* too; nay, that is not sufficient neither; you must have the reputation of them also.

Your character in the world must be built upon that solid foundation, or it will soon fall, and upon your own head. You cannot, therefore, be too careful, too nice, too scrupulous, in establishing this character at first, upon which your whole depends. Let no conversation, no example, no fashion, no *bon mot*, no silly desire of seeming to be above what most knaves and many fools call prejudices, ever tempt you to avow, excuse, extenuate, or laugh at the least breach of morality; but show upon all occasions, and take all occasions to show, a detestation and abhorrence of it. There, though young, you ought to be strict; and there only, while young, it becomes you to be strict and severe. But there too, spare the persons while you lash the crimes. All this relates, as you easily judge, to the vices of the heart, such as lying, fraud, envy, malice, detraction, etc.; and I do not extend it to the little frailties of youth, flowing from high spirits and warm blood. It would ill become you, at your age, to declaim against them, and sententiously censure a gallantry, an accidental excess of the table, a frolic, an inadvertency; no, keep as free from them yourself as you can, but say nothing against them in others. They certainly mend by time, often by reason; and a man's worldly character is not affected by them, provided it be pure in all other respects.

For God's sake, revolve all these things seriously in

Recollect the observations that you have yourself made upon mankind, compare and connect them with my instructions, and then act systematically and consequentially from them. Lay your little plan now.

your thoughts before you launch out alone into the ocean of Paris. Recollect the observations that you have yourself made upon mankind, compare and connect them with my instructions, and then act systematically and consequentially from them; not *au jour la journée.* Lay your little plan now, which you will hereafter extend and improve by your own observations, and by the advice of those who can never mean to mislead you; I mean Mr. Harte and myself. Adieu!

Dear Boy,   *January, 1750*
    I have seldom or never written to you upon the subject of Religion and Morality: your own reason, I am persuaded, has given you true notions of both; they speak best for themselves; but, if they wanted assistance, you have Mr. Harte at hand, both for precept and example; to your own reason, therefore, and to Mr. Harte, shall I refer you, for the reality of both; and

confine myself, in this letter, to the decency, the utility, and the necessity, of scrupulously preserving the appearances of both. When I say the appearances of religion, I do not mean that you should talk or act like a missionary, or an enthusiast, nor that you should take up a controversial cudgel against whoever attacks the sect you are of; this would be both useless and unbecoming your age; but I mean that you should by no means seem to approve, encourage, or applaud, those libertine notions, which strike at religions equally, and which are the poor threadbare topics of half wits, and minute philosophers. Even those who are silly enough to laugh at their jokes, are still wise enough to distrust and detest their characters; for, putting moral virtues at the highest, and religion at the lowest, religion must still be allowed to be a collateral security, at least, to virtue; and every prudent man will sooner trust to two securities than to one.

Whenever, therefore, you happen to be in company with those pretended *esprits forts*, or with thoughtless libertines, who laugh at all religion, to show their wit, or disclaim it, to complete their riot; let no word or look of yours intimate the least approbation; on the contrary, let a silent gravity express your dislike; but enter not into the subject, and decline such unprofitable and indecent controversies. Depend upon this truth, That every man is the worse looked upon, and the less trusted, for being thought to have no religion; in spite of all the pompous and specious epithets he may assume, of *esprit fort*, freethinker, or moral philosopher; and a wise atheist (if such a thing there is) would, for his own interest, and character in this world, pretend to some religion.

Your moral character must be not only pure, but, like Cæsar's wife, unsuspected. The least speck or blemish upon it is fatal. Nothing degrades and vilifies more, for it excites and unites detestation and contempt. There are, however, wretches in the world profligate enough to explode' all notions of moral good and evil; to maintain that they are merely local, and depend entirely upon the customs and fashions of different countries; nay, there are still, if possible, more unaccountable wretches; I mean those who affect to preach and propagate such absurd and infamous notions, without believing them themselves. These are the devil's hypocrites. Avoid as much as possible the company of such people, who reflect a degree of discredit and infamy upon all who converse with them. But as you may, sometimes, by accident, fall into such company, take great care that no complaisance, no good-humour, no warmth of festal mirth, ever make you seem even to acquiesce, much less to approve or applaud, such infamous doctrines. On the other hand; do not debate, nor enter into serious argument, upon a subject so much below it: but content yourself with telling those *Apostles*, that you know they are not serious; that you have a much better opinion of them than they would have you have; and that, you are very sure, they would not practise the doctrine they preach. But put your private mark upon them, and shun them for ever afterwards.

THE ART OF PERFORMANCE

CHAPTER

10

I n classical times, rhetoric was the art of speaking well, with the specific aim of persuasion. Language was codified into a series of rules, and there was a sense in which the speaker didn't so much express his thoughts, as arrange them in patterns. Some philosophers regarded rhetoric with suspicion, since it placed too great an emphasis on the effect of language, and opened up possibilities for manipulating the truth inherent in the meaning of the words themselves. Actors, evangelists, politicians, all use rhetoric, and clearly for Chesterfield, it is the summation of his system – the final, most practical aspect for a son destined for Parliament, of a strategy dedicated to 'substance' and 'mode'.

Speech, as he notes, is the sign of man's civilisation, the basis of communication, the vehicle for sociability and human intercourse. In this context, 'substance' comprises the words, and many of the ideas about letter writing, discussed in Chapter 7, apply once more. Choice of words is of paramount importance. Ambiguity is merely inefficient, and Chesterfield censures all forms of linguistic impropriety – poor grammar, redundant phrases, loose usage. This is the bedrock on which the performance art of rhetoric will be built.

'Mode' is the performance art itself, the ability to conjure up a mental perception which carries belief, and is thus other than literal understanding. In his letter describing how he convinced the House of Lords to adopt for the country a new calendar, Chesterfield shows how to convince an audience unlikely to be held by a thoroughgoing analysis of a complex subject, both that he had command of that subject and that nothing had been denied them in his speaking of it. 'They thought I informed, because I pleased them; and many of them said, that I had made the whole very clear to them, when, God knows, I had not even attempted it.'

Dear Boy,   *November, 1739*

Let us return to Oratory, or the art of speaking well; which should never be entirely out of your thoughts, since it is so useful in every part of life, and so absolutely necessary in most. A man can make no figure without it, in Parliament, in the Church, or in the law; and even in common conversation, a man that has acquired an easy and habitual eloquence, who speaks properly and accurately, will have a great advantage over those who speak incorrectly or inelegantly.

The business of Oratory, as I have told you before, is to persuade people; and you easily feel, that to please people is a great step towards persuading them. You must then, consequently, be sensible how advantageous it is for a man who speaks in public, whether it be in Parliament, or in the pulpit, or at the bar (that is, in the courts of law), to please his hearers so much as to gain their attention; which he can never do without the help of oratory. It is not enough to speak the language he speaks in, in its utmost purity, and according to the rules of grammar, but he must speak it elegantly, that is, he must use the best and the most expressive words, and put them in the best order. He should likewise adorn what he says by proper metaphors, similes, and the other figures of rhetoric; and he should enliven it, if he can, by quick and sprightly turns of wit. For example, supposing you had a mind to persuade Mr. Maittaire to give you a holiday, would you bluntly say to him, "Give me a holiday"? That would certainly not be the way to persuade him to it. But you should endeavour first to please him, and gain his attention, by telling him, that your experience of his goodness and indulgence encouraged you to ask a favour of him; that, if he should not think proper to grant it, at least you hoped he would not take it ill that you asked it.

Then you should tell him what it was you wanted; that it was a holiday, for which you should give your reasons, as that you had such and such a thing to do, or such a place to go to. Then you might urge some argument, why he should not refuse you; as, that you have seldom asked the favour, and that you seldom will; and that the mind may sometimes require a little rest from labour as well as the body. This you may illustrate by a simile, and say, that as the bow is the stronger for being sometimes unstrung and unbent, so the mind will be capable of more attention for being now and then easy and relaxed.

This is a little oration, fit for such a little orator as you; but, however, it will make you understand what is meant by oratory and eloquence; which is to persuade. I hope you will have that talent hereafter in great matters. Adieu

Dear Boy,   *November, 1749*
Every rational being (I take it for granted) proposes to himself some object more important than mere respiration and obscure animal existence. He desires to distinguish himself among his fellow-creatures; and, *alicui negotio intentus, præclari facinoris, aut artis bonæ,*

famam qærit. Cæsar, when embarking in a storm, said, that it was not necessary he should live; but that it was absolutely necessary he should get to the place to which he was going. And Pliny leaves mankind this only alternative; either of doing what deserves to be written, or of writing what deserves to be read. As for those who do neither, *eorum vitam mortemque juxta æstumo; quoniam de utrâque siletur.* You have, I am convinced, one or both of these objects in view; but you must know, and use the necessary means, or your pursuit will be vain and frivolous. In either case, *sapere est principium et fons*; but it is by no means all. That knowledge may be adorned, it must have lustre as well as weight, or it will be oftener taken for lead than for gold. Knowledge you have, and will have; I am easy upon that article. But my business, as your friend, is not to compliment you upon what you have, but to tell you with freedom what you want; and I must tell you plainly, that I fear you want everything but knowledge.

I have written to you so often of late upon good-breeding, address, *les manières liantes*, the Graces, etc., that I shall confine this letter to another subject, pretty near akin to them, and which, I am sure, you are full as deficient in—I mean style.

Style is the dress of thoughts; and let them be ever so just, if your style is homely, coarse, and vulgar, they will appear to as much disadvantage, and be as ill received as your person, though ever so well proportioned, would, if dressed in rags, dirt, and tatters. It is not every understanding that can judge of matter, but every ear can and does judge, more or less, of style; and were I either to speak or write to the public, I should prefer moderate matter, adorned with all the beauties and elegances of style, to the strongest matter in the world, ill-worded and ill-delivered. Your business is negotiation abroad, and oratory in the House of Commons at home. What figure can you make in either case, if your style be inelegant, I do not say bad? Imagine yourself writing an office-letter to a Secretary of State, which letter is to be read by the whole Cabinet Council, and very possibly afterwards laid before Parliament; any one barbarism, solecism, or vulgarism in it would, in a very few days, circulate through the whole kingdom, to your disgrace and ridicule. For instance; I will suppose you had written the following letter from the Hague, to the Secretary of State at London; and leave you to suppose the consequences of it.

My Lord,

I *had*, last night, the honour of your Lordship's letter of the 24th; and will *set about doing* the orders contained *therein*; and *if so be* that I can get that affair done by the next post, I will not fail *for to* give your Lordship an account of it by *next post*. I have told the French Minister, *as how, that if* that affair be not soon concluded, your Lordship would think it *all long of him*; and that he must have neglected *for to* have wrote to his Court about it. I must beg leave to put your Lordship in mind, *as how*, that I am now full three quarters in arrear; and if *so be* that I do not very soon receive at least one half year, I shall *cut a very bad figure*; for *this here* place is very dear. I shall be *vastly beholden* to your Lordship for *that there* mark of your favour; and so I *rest*, or *remain*, Your etc.

You will tell me, possibly, that this is a *caricatura* of an illiberal and inelegant style; I will admit it; but assure you, at the same time, that a despatch with less than half these faults would blow you up for ever. It is by no means sufficient to be free from faults in speaking and writing; you must do both correctly and elegantly. In faults of this kind, it is not *ille optimus qui minimis urgetur*, but he is unpardonable who has any at all, because it is his own fault; he need only attend to, observe, and imitate the best authors.

It is a very true saying, that a man must be born a poet, but that he may make himself an orator; and the very first principle of an orator is, to speak his own language particularly, with the utmost purity and elegancy. A man will be forgiven, even great errors, in a foreign language; but in his own, even the least slips are justly laid hold of and ridiculed.

Gain the heart, or you gain nothing; the eyes and the ears are the only roads to the heart.

Constant experience has shown me, that great purity and elegance of style, with a graceful elocution, cover a multitude of faults, in either a speaker or a writer. For my own part, I confess (and I believe most people are of my mind) that if a speaker should ungracefully mutter or stammer out to me the sense of an angel, deformed by barbarisms and solecisms, or larded with vulgarisms, he should never speak to me a second time, if I could help it. Gain the heart, or you gain nothing; the eyes and the ears are the only roads to the heart. Merit and knowledge will not gain hearts, though they will secure them when gained. Pray have that truth ever in your mind. Engage the eyes by your address, air, and motions; soothe the ears, by the elegancy and harmony of your diction; the heart will certainly follow; and the whole man, or woman, will as certainly follow the heart. I must repeat it to you, over and over again, that, with all the knowledge which you may have at present, or hereafter acquire, and with all the merit that ever man had, if you have not a graceful address, liberal and engaging manners, a prepossessing air, and a good degree of eloquence in speaking and writing, you will be nobody; but will have the daily mortification of seeing people, with not one-tenth part of your merit or knowledge, get the start of you, and disgrace you both in company and in business.

You have read Quintilian; the best book in the world to form an orator: pray read *Cicero de Oratore*; the best book in the world to finish one. Translate and retranslate, from and to Latin, Greek, and English; make yourself a pure and elegant English style; it requires nothing but application. I do not find that God has made you a poet; and I am very glad that He has not; therefore, for God's sake, make yourself an orator, which you may do. Though I still call you boy, I consider you no longer as such; and when I reflect upon the prodigious quantity of manure that has been laid upon you, I expect you should produce more at eighteen, than uncultivated soils do at eight-and-twenty.

Dear Boy,   *December, 1749*
   I have spoken frequently in Parliament, and not always without some applause; and therefore I can assure you, from my experience, that there is very little in it. The elegancy of the style, and the turn of the periods, make the chief impression upon the hearers. Give them but one or two round and harmonious periods in a speech, which they will retain and repeat, and they will go home as well satisfied, as people do from an opera, humming all the way one or two favourite tunes that have struck their ears and were

Most people have ears, but few have judgment; tickle those ears, and, depend upon it, you will catch their judgments such as they are.

easily caught. Most people have ears, but few have judgment; tickle those ears, and, depend upon it, you will catch their judgments, such as they are.
   Cicero, conscious that he was at the top of his profession (for in his time eloquence was a profession), in order to set himself off, defines, in his treatise *de Oratore*, an orator to be such a man as never was, or never will be; and by this fallacious argument, says, that he must know every art and science whatsoever, or how

shall he speak upon them? But with submission to so great an authority, my definition of an orator is extremely different from, and, I believe, much truer than his. I call that man an orator, who reasons justly, and expresses himself elegantly upon whatever subject he treats. Problems in geometry, equations in algebra, processes in chymistry, and experiments in anatomy, are never, that I have heard of, the objects of eloquence; and therefore I humbly conceive, that a man may be a very fine speaker, and yet know nothing of geometry, algebra, chymistry, or anatomy. The subjects of all parliamentary debates, are subjects of common sense singly.

Thus I write whatever occurs to me, that I may contribute either to form or inform you. May my labour not be in vain! and it will not, if you will but have half the concern for yourself, that I have for you. Adieu!

Dear Boy,   *December, 1749*

You will be of the House of Commons as soon as you are of age; and you must first make a figure there, if you would make a figure, or a fortune, in your country. This you can never do without that correctness and elegancy in your own language, which you now seem to neglect, and which you have entirely to learn. Fortunately for you, it is to be learned. Care and observation will do it; but do not flatter yourself, that all the knowledge, sense, and reasoning in the world will ever make you a popular and applauded speaker, without the ornaments and the graces, of style, elocution, and action. Sense and argument, though coarsely delivered, will have their weight in a private conversation, with two or three people of sense; but in a public assembly they will have none, if naked and destitute of the advantages I have mentioned. Cardinal de Retz observes, very justly, that every numerous assembly is mob, influenced by their passions, humours, and affections, which nothing but eloquence ever did, or ever can engage. This is so important a consideration for every body in this country, and more particularly for you, that I earnestly recommend it to your most serious care and attention.

Mind your diction, in whatever language you either write or speak; contract a habit of correctness and elegance. Consider your style, even in the freest conversation, and most familiar letters. After, at least, if not before you have said a thing, reflect if you could not have said it better. Where you doubt of the propriety or elegancy of a word or a phrase, consult some good dead or living authority in that language. Use yourself to translate from various languages into English; correct those translations till they satisfy your ear, as well as your understanding. And be convinced of this truth, That the best sense and reason in the world will be as unwelcome in a public assembly, without these ornaments, as they will in public companies, without the assistance of manners and politeness. If you will please people, you must please them in their own way; and as you cannot make them what they should be, you must take them as they are. I repeat it again, they are only to be taken by *agrémens*, and by what flatters their senses and their hearts. Rabelais first wrote a most excellent book, which nobody liked; then, determined to conform to the public taste, he wrote *Gargantua and Pantagruel*, which everybody liked, extravagant as it was. Adieu!

'When you come into the House of Commons, if you imagine that speaking plain and unadorned sense and reason will do your business, you will find yourself grossly mistaken.'

Dear Boy,   *March, 1751*

I acquainted you in a former letter that I had brought a bill into the House of Lords, for correcting and reforming our present calendar, which is the Julian, and for adopting the Gregorian. I will now give you a more particular account of that affair, from which reflections will naturally occur to you that I hope may be useful, and which I fear you have not made. It was notorious, that the Julian calendar was erroneous, and had overcharged the solar year with eleven days. Pope Gregory XIII corrected this error; his reformed calendar was immediately received by all the Catholic Powers of Europe, and afterwards adopted by all the Protestant ones, except Russia, Sweden, and England. It was not, in my opinion, very honourable for England to remain in a gross and avowed error, especially in such company; the inconvenience of it was likewise felt by all those who had foreign correspondences, whether political or mercantile. I determined, therefore, to attempt the reformation; I consulted the best lawyers, and the most skilful astronomers, and we cooked up a bill for that purpose. But then my difficulty began; I was to bring in this bill, which was necessarily composed of law jargon and astronomical calculations, to both which I am an utter stranger. However, it was absolutely necessary to make the House of Lords think that I knew something of the matter, and also to make them believe that they knew something of it themselves, which they do not. For my own part, I could just as soon have talked Celtic or Sclavonian to them as astronomy, and they would have understood me full as well; so I resolved to do better than speak to the purpose, and to please instead of informing them. I gave them, therefore, only an historical account of calendars, from the Egyptian down to the Gregorian, amusing them now and then with little episodes; but I was particularly attentive to the choice of my words, to the harmony and roundness of my periods, to my elocution, to my action. This succeeded, and ever will succeed; they thought I informed, because I pleased them; and many of them said, that I had made the whole very clear to them, when, God knows, I had not even attempted it. Lord Macclesfield, who had the greatest share in forming the bill, and who is one of the greatest mathematicians and astronomers in Europe, spoke afterwards with infinite knowledge, and all the clearness that so intricate a matter would admit of; but as his words, his periods, and his utterance were not near so good as mine, the preference was most unanimously, though most unjustly, given to me.

This will ever be the case; every numerous assembly is *mob*, let the individuals who compose it be what they will. Mere reason and good sense is never to be talked to a mob; their passions, their sentiments, their senses, and their seeming interests, are alone to be applied to. Understanding they have collectively none; but they have ears and eyes, which must be flattered and seduced; and this can only be done by eloquence, tuneful periods, graceful action, and all the various parts of oratory.

When you come into the House of Commons, if you imagine that speaking plain and unadorned sense and reason will do your business, you will find yourself mostly grossly mistaken. As a speaker, you will be ranked only according to your eloquence, and by no

When you come into the House of Commons, if you imagine that speaking plain and unadorned sense and reason will do your business, you will find yourself grossly mistaken.

means according to your matter; everybody knows the matter almost alike, but few can adorn it. I was early convinced of the importance and powers of eloquence, and from that moment I applied myself to it. I resolved not to utter one word, even in common conversation, that should not be the most expressive and the most elegant that the language could supply me with for that purpose; by which means I have acquired such a certain degree of habitual eloquence, that I must now really take some pains, if I would express myself very inelegantly. I want to inculcate this known truth into you, which you seem by no means to be convinced of yet—that ornaments are at present your only objects. Your sole business now is to shine, not to weigh. Weight without lustre is lead. You had better talk trifles elegantly, to the most trifling woman, than coarse inelegant sense to the most solid man. You had better return a dropped fan genteelly, than give a thousand pounds awkwardly; and you had better refuse a favour gracefully, than grant it clumsily. Manner is all in everything; it is by manner only that you can please, and consequently rise. All your Greek will never advance you from Secretary to Envoy, or from Envoy to Ambassador; but your address, your manner, your air, if good, very probably may. Marcel can be of much more use to you than Aristotle. I would, upon my word, much rather that you had Lord Bolingbroke's style and eloquence, in speaking and writing, than all the learning of the Academy of Sciences, the Royal Society, and the two Universities united.

Having mentioned Lord Bolingbroke's style, which is, undoubtedly, infinitely superior to anybody's, I would have you read his works, which you have, over and over again, with particular attention to his style. Transcribe, imitate, emulate it, if possible; that would be of real use to you in the House of Commons, in negotiations, in conversation; with that, you may justly hope to please, to persuade, to seduce, to impose; and you will fail in those articles, in proportion as you fall short of it. Upon the whole, lay aside, during your year's residence at Paris, all thoughts of all that dull fellows call solid, and exert your utmost care to acquire what people of fashion call shining. *Prenez l'éclat et le brilliant d'un galant homme.*

My Dear Friend,   *February, 1751*

When you go to the play, which I hope you do often, for it is a very instructive amusement, you must certainly have observed the very different effects which the several parts have upon you, according as they are well or ill acted. The very best tragedy of Corneille's, if well spoken and acted, interests, engages, agitates, and affects your passions. Love, terror, and pity, alternately possess you. But if ill spoken and acted, it would only excite your indignation or your laughter. Why? It is still Corneille's; it is the same sense, the same matter, whether well or ill acted. It is then merely the manner of speaking and acting that makes this great difference in the effects. Apply this to yourself, and conclude from it, that if you would either please in a private company, or persuade in a public assembly, air, looks, gestures, graces, enunciation, proper accents, just emphasis, and tuneful cadences, are full as necessary as the matter itself. Let awkward, ungraceful, inelegant, and dull fellows say what they will in behalf of their solid matter and strong reasonings, and let them despise all those graces and ornaments, which engage the senses and captivate the heart; they will find (though they will possible wonder why) that their rough unpolished matter, and their unadorned, coarse, but strong arguments, will neither please nor persuade, but, on the contrary, will tire our attention and excite disgust. We are so made, we love to be pleased better than to be informed; information is, in a certain degree, mortifying, as it implies our previous ignorance; it must be sweetened to be palatable.

The same thing holds full as true in conversation, where even trifles, elegantly expressed, well looked, and accompanied with graceful action, will ever please, beyond all the home-spun, unadorned sense in the world. Reflect, on one side, how you feel within yourself, while you are forced to suffer the tedious, muddy, and ill-turned narration of some awkward fellow, even though the fact may be interesting; and on the other hand, with what pleasure you attend to the relation of a much less interesting matter, when elegantly expressed, genteelly turned, and gracefully delivered. By attending carefully to all these *agrémens* in your daily conversation, they will become habitual to you, before you come into Parliament; and you will have nothing then to do but to raise them a little when you come there. I would wish you to be so attentive to this object, that I would not have you speak to your footman but in the very best words that the subject admits of, be the language which it will. Think of your words, and of their arrangement, before you speak; choose the most elegant, and place them in the best order. Consult your own ear, to avoid cacophony; and what is very near as bad, monotony. Think also of your gesture and looks, when you are speaking even upon the most trifling subjects. The same things differently expressed, looked, and delivered, cease to be the same things. The most passionate lover in the world cannot make a stronger declaration of love than the *Bourgeois Gentilhomme* does in this happy form of words, *Mourir d'amour me font belle Marquise vos beaux yeux*. I defy anybody to say more; and yet I would advise nobody to say that; and I would recommend to you rather to smother and conceal your passion entirely than to reveal it in these words. Seriously, this holds in everything, as well as in that ludicrous instance. The French, to do them justice, attend very minutely to the purity, the correctness and the elegancy of their style, in conversation, and in their letters. *Bien narrer* is an object of their study; and though they sometimes carry it to affectation, they never sink into inelegancy, which is much the worst extreme of the two. Observe them, and form your French style upon